The New Seoul Park Jelly Massacre

CHO YEEUN

Translated by Yewon Jung

Honford Star

This translation first published by Honford Star 2024

Honford Star Ltd.
Profolk, Bank Chambers
Stockport
SK1 1AR
honfordstar.com

뉴서울파크 젤리장수 대학살
New Seoul Park Jelly Vendor Massacre by Cho Yeeun
Copyright © 2019 Cho Yeeun
English translation copyright © Safehouse Inc.
English edition is published by arrangement with Safehouse Inc.
through AMO Agency Korea
All rights reserved.

ISBN (paperback): 978-1-915829-03-0
ISBN (ebook): 978-1-915829-04-7
A catalogue record for this book is available from the British Library.

Printed and bound in Paju, South Korea
Cover art by Jee-ook Choi
Typeset by Honford Star
Cover paper: 250 gsm Vent Nouveau by TAKEO, Japan
Endleaves: 116 gsm NT Rasha by TAKEO, Japan

1 3 5 7 9 10 8 6 4 2

Contents

1. *The Missing Child* — 5
2. *The Survivor* — 33
3. *The Mascot Cat* — 69
4. *Our First Day Together* — 77
5. *Two Hundred Meters to the Hamster Wheel* — 103
6. *The Sabbath* — 115
7. *Friends without Names* — 155
8. *New Seoul Park* — 191
9. *The Missing Child* — 201

The Missing Child

Yuji stared at the top of the ride as it soared up into the sky. The sound of people screaming came from nearby, then far away, then nearby again. The Drop Tower standing before her was supposed to be the scariest ride in New Seoul Park. The donut-shaped structure spiraled slowly up to the top, before dropping to the bottom in an instant. The people on the ride enjoyed the excitement, relying on nothing but a safety bar for their lives. Yuji wondered what the suspense felt like. People said the terror gave you a big thrill.

It was something Yuji wasn't able to experience for herself. Crestfallen, she hung her head. She had told everyone in her class about her big plans, never imagining that she wouldn't be able to go on the ride because she wasn't tall enough, falling short by one centimeter. *Well, too bad*, she thought. Yuji decided to go on another ride she had in mind and looked around for her parents.

Her parents were standing face to face under a wisteria tree far away. It seemed they were arguing again, waving their hands in the air and yelling. They didn't get on very well. They were always saying mean things to each other and quarreling and throwing stuff around over what seemed like little things to Yuji. On rare quiet days, they didn't say a word to each other.

Yuji pursed her lips. Here they were at a fun and exciting theme park, and her parents were busy fighting again. Only one person in the world could pacify this problematic couple.

"Mom! Dad! I want to go on a different ride," Yuji shouted in a cheerful voice. The couple, who had been seething with rage, finally relaxed and smiled at Yuji.

With a proud smile on her face, Yuji said, "I wonder how you guys will ever get on without me. Who's the parent here, huh?"

Yuji shook her head, imitating the way grown-ups spoke. Her mom stopped glaring at her dad and came up to her and took her hand. Yuji thrust her other hand at her dad. Sighing, her dad also took her hand.

The theme park in mid-August felt like a steamer packed with dumplings. The spacious park was crammed full of people. Beads of sweat rolled down from Yuji's round forehead. Yuji's parents were sweating as well. Both of the hands Yuji was holding were damp with sweat. It seemed her dad wanted to pull his hand away, but Yuji pretended not to notice. She didn't like the dampness either, but she was afraid that her mom and dad would scatter away and disappear the moment she let go of their hands. Yuji tightened her grip on her dad's hand. The three of them were together, her mom in one hand, her dad in the other. Yuji had a picture of the perfect family in her mind.

Yuji's gaze fell on something: Dream Teddy handing out balloons in front of the carousel in the main square of the park.

Dream Teddy, along with Dream Kitty, was the mascot of New Seoul Park; Dream Teddy, the guardian of New Seoul Park and the everlasting friend of children. Yuji began to hum Teddy's theme song, which she had heard too many times on television.

Yuji liked Dream Teddy. Some kids in her class called Teddy a mutt, saying he was a mixture of several different characters from overseas, but Yuji didn't care. She felt happy when she saw Teddy's plastic eyes, sparkling so brightly that they almost made him look idiotic, and his bulging belly. Yuji felt that Teddy would nod his head eagerly at her, no matter what she said to him.

"Do you want a balloon?" her mom asked quickly. Yuji nodded in reply.

"Well, then, go and get one. Go and say, a balloon, please!" her mom said, her hand slipping out of Yuji's as if it had just been waiting for the chance.

Yuji looked at her mom. The corners of her mouth turning up in a smile, her mom gave Yuji a gentle push. Yuji's dad was fanning himself with the hand he had already pulled away. Yuji stared at her own hands, suddenly empty. She wanted to grab onto something, anything. She kept clenching and unclenching her fists, but she couldn't shake the feeling of emptiness. Finally, she went up to Dream Teddy. As she reached out a hand toward the balloons, a group of kids came out of nowhere and shoved past her.

The kids, who seemed to be on a group trip, cut in line like a swarm of bees and snatched away the balloons. When Yuji's turn came at last, there wasn't a single balloon left. Dream Teddy shrugged, waving his hands, as if to say there was nothing he could do. Yuji turned around with a prim look on her face.

She couldn't let herself get upset over something like this. Whining about not getting a balloon was a childish thing to do. Yuji was very mature for her age—a grown-up, in fact, who could calm her parents who fought like little kids. Yuji straightened her back and turned in the direction of her parents. They had seized the opportunity to get themselves into another quarrel. Music—more like noise, actually—rang throughout the park, but she could still somehow clearly hear the sound of her parents fighting.

"A theme park, in this heat—it's insane! Did we really have to come, just because she wanted to? Can't I get some rest on the weekend, at least?"

"Well, what could we do? She wanted to come. Do you ever pay any attention to what she wants?"

"It wasn't because I wanted to come," Yuji mumbled in a small voice, coming to a stop.

About a week ago, Yuji had been watching television when a commercial came on, promoting New Seoul Park's summer special late-night package. Her mom, sitting on the floor folding laundry, suddenly said to herself, "It's been ages since I've been someplace like that."

Her mom never went anywhere but work; her life seemed stifling even to Yuji. After some thought, she had asked her dad secretly when her mom wasn't home, "Have you ever been to a theme park?"

"Of course, when I was young. Good old days," her dad had replied, his eyes sparkling for a moment. Had he enjoyed it that much? So why didn't he just go again? It wasn't like theme parks had an age restriction. Yuji thought that she should help out her mom and dad. When they were both home and the television commercial came on again, she had said in a chirpy voice, "I wish I could go to a theme park. Most of the kids in my class have been to one."

That was how they'd ended up coming to New Seoul Park. She did say that she wanted to come, but not because she really wanted to; she had brought it up because she thought her parents wanted to come. She had no idea that her dad had come so grudgingly. His words hurt her feelings and annoyed her. She'd had a different picture in mind. She thought that her parents would be happier if they, like so many other families, spent time together going on childish but cute rides and eating sweets.

With her parents quarreling in front of her, Yuji turned away. She hated them for always fighting and for being oblivious to all the efforts their daughter was making. When she raised her head, she noticed a sign saying, 200 METERS TO THE HAMSTER WHEEL. The quarrel grew more and more heated. Yuji heaved a deep sigh that was too grave for a child. Then she followed the arrow to the path leading to the Hamster Wheel.

The Hamster Wheel was the second most famous ride in New Seoul Park, the first being the Drop Tower. The Hamster Wheel wasn't a scary ride in itself, but it had become famous as a "ride of terror" because of its violent spinning—as if it had a screw missing—and the rumors about accidents, groundless as they were. Getting on the wheel would be something to brag about to her classmates. Plus it didn't have a height restriction. Following the sparsely placed arrows, Yuji made her way deeper into the park.

The Hamster Wheel was in a remote corner of the park. Unlike the main square, which was packed with crowds, this part of the park was strangely empty. After walking for a good while, Yuji saw a colorful cone-shaped roof in the distance. Still no sign of people, though. Puzzled, Yuji went up to the ride.

The waiting area for the ride was locked up in chains. Above the chains hung a sign that said UNDER REPAIR.

"So annoying," Yuji said, as she hunkered down and leaned against the fence. Why had she come all the way here? She should have realized that there was a reason for no one being here. The thought of making her way back without getting anything out of her long walk was discouraging. But there was nothing else to be done. Yuji got back on her feet. The small backpack she was carrying felt awfully heavy. All she could do in the end, though, was shoot the innocent Hamster Wheel a fierce look before heading back toward the main square.

Sweat poured down her forehead and back. The heat was so intense that she felt like she would melt. She hadn't realized how hot this summer really was, as her school and after-school academy were always cold with air conditioning. The heat also made her quite irritable.

She hadn't been able to go on any of the rides she had looked forward to, and her parents were just busy fighting. Yuji felt sad, as it seemed that they didn't even want to hold hands with her. But as always, she had to be understanding, as she was the mature one. *I'll just suggest that we go have some smoothies at a café,* she thought. As she walked, she heard an unfamiliar voice call out from a corner.

"Hi," said the voice.

The New Seoul Park Jelly Massacre

Yuji turned her head. A man in an old uniform had come out of nowhere and was beckoning at her. Yuji tilted her head. There hadn't been anyone there, she was sure of that. Yuji turned around to face him, and the man, slowly shaking a packet of jelly in his other hand, said, "Want some jelly?"

Only then did she notice a mobile stall laden with countless packets of jelly. Yuji's mouth watered. She had, in fact, been craving something sweet for a while. Lunch had been a children's meal—unappetizing and small—at the park cafeteria. She had seen other people with churros or cotton candy, but she hadn't asked her mom to buy her anything; pestering your parents for sweets was a childish thing to do.

Yuji replied from a distance, "I don't spend money on sweets."

The man smiled and said, "You don't have to spend money on them. They're free samples because this jelly just came out. Want to try some?"

Yuji felt tempted. *Mom and Dad are probably still fighting*, she thought. *Wouldn't it be all right to take some, since they're free?* Yuji went up to the man. He was wearing a yellow-green hat, part of the uniform, low on his head. Yuji couldn't see his face very well for some reason, even though she was looking right up at him. It was as if his face was smeared with mud. As Yuji approached him, he handed her a packet of jelly and whispered, "You don't want to be apart from your parents, do you?"

Yuji opened her eyes wide and asked, "How did you know?"

"Because I can see them fighting from here," he said.

Yuji whirled around. No matter how much she craned her neck to try and see her parents, the main square was out of her view. The man seemed kind of weird. Or maybe he had seen her parents fighting when he was around the main square. Still, it was strange that he would make a point of telling her that.

Thinking she should hurry back, Yuji took the packet of jelly. The man's fingertips felt cold, like the skin of her friend's pet turtle. The strange sensation made her shake off his hand instinctively. Unperturbed, he grinned and said, "If you share the jelly with your parents, they will never split up."

Yuji crumpled up the packet in her hand. Feeling uneasy, she turned around and bolted. She felt as though she had dipped her feet in a dark, sticky puddle. The man's laugh followed her like an echo.

Only when she had come back out to the main square did she realize that the air around the man had been unnaturally cool. Standing under the scorching sun now, with no shade anywhere, she began to sweat once again. Having lost her appetite, she put the packet of jelly in her backpack.

She wanted something cool to drink. She looked around for her parents. The two had until a little while ago been quarreling under the wisteria tree but were now nowhere to be seen. Yuji looked up at the clock tower. It had taken only ten minutes for her to make her way to the Hamster Wheel and back. Ten minutes wasn't enough time for them to go far away without her. Yuji hovered around the square. Dream Teddy was still dancing to the music like a ballerina in a music box, and the carousel was still moving at its tedious, constant pace. The sign saying HAMSTER WHEEL was still in place, and so was the enormous clock tower. Only her parents were gone. They had disappeared.

"Mom! Dad!" Yuji shouted, going wherever her feet took her. Before she knew it, the Drop Tower was standing in front of her.

The New Seoul Park Jelly Massacre

People stared at her. It seemed they felt sorry for her. The day was still hot and her throat was parched. She just wanted to go home now. She wanted to go home and have some ice-cold water. She came to a sudden stop and stood there thinking. Her parents had probably gone off looking for her. If so, what would be the easiest way for them to find her? As she pondered, she caught sight of a sign that read LOST CHILDREN CENTER.

The Lost Children Center was in the shape of a red mushroom. *Red mushrooms are poisonous,* Yuji thought, recalling what she had read in a book. She entered the mushroom house. An employee wearing bunny ears came up to her and asked some questions. Yuji answered as coherently as she could.

It was chaotic inside the booth. Kids younger than Yuji, and even some who looked older, were crying and screaming. *So childish,* Yuji thought. When she had answered all the questions, the employee smiled and said, "If you sit over there and wait with the others, your parents will come get you soon."

She didn't like being grouped together with the savage kids, but she didn't let on. She nodded and sat down in an empty chair. *Soon, soon,* she repeated in her mind. Her parents, however, still hadn't shown up after an hour. And there at the center, she met Jua.

*

Jua was a girl who cried a lot. She cried for a whole hour after coming into the Lost Children Center. Yuji, feeling awkward for sitting close by and not doing anything, pulled out some wet wipes from her backpack and handed them to her. Blinking her large eyes, Jua began to sob even more loudly. Then she mumbled in a garbled voice, "My mom must have abandoned me. I kept asking for an expensive toy, even though we don't have any money."

"Don't cry. She'll come for you."

"No, she won't. I hate her!" Jua cried, pulling the conch-shaped hairpin out of her hair and hurling it on the floor. The purple hairpin, bouncing off the floor, ended up under a chair. Jua looked at it with regret, though she had thrown it herself.

Jua picked up the pin, then flung it to the floor again; she kept on doing this over and over. She seemed quite confused. Without a word, Yuji dusted off Jua's knees. Yuji's mom also sometimes threw stuff around while crying.

Yuji sat there comforting Jua for a long time. She didn't say anything particularly kind or warm—she just told Jua not to cry and handed her some tissues. Still, Jua must have found Yuji friendly and affectionate, as she was leaning comfortably on her shoulder now. Jua's tears continued to pour like an ever-flowing fountain.

Yuji found it incredible that someone could cry with such great sorrow. She felt somewhat proud, though, that she—being mature—was taking care of a childish little girl. Children who were mature for their age always helped those in need of comfort. When her mom came for her, Yuji would tell her what happened. *She'll compliment me,* she thought. She wondered how she could tell her about all the troubles she'd been through without sounding like a baby.

Time went by, and the kids who had been kicking up a fuss each left with his or her parents. Yuji grew anxious as the red mushroom house became increasingly quiet. Three hours had passed already. She flinched every time the door opened and checked to see who was there, only to find a stranger standing there each time. Jua seemed tired, too—she had stopped crying and just sat there blinking her round eyes.

An employee came cautiously up to Yuji and handed her a piece of paper. There were blanks to be filled in with information that included her name, age, school, and home address. Yuji filled in as many blanks as she could. All she could remember of her address was "P Apartments, Building Two." She had her full address memorized, but for some reason she couldn't recall it. It was frustrating. She felt as if something sticky was wrapped around her brain so that it couldn't function properly. Was it because she was anxious?

Jua wrote down her mom's name, but then began to sniffle again, saying she couldn't remember her address. Several announcements went out, but Yuji's parents did not show up.

Yuji whispered to Jua, "Let's get out of here. We need to go look for them ourselves."

Jua asked through a runny nose, "Do you think we can find them?"

"It's better than just sitting here waiting around."

Jua gave a loud sniffle and nodded her head. The two waited for their chance, and when the employee was momentarily distracted, they ducked and rushed out. Once outside, the humid heat once again enveloped them. Their skin, cooled from the air conditioning, heated up instantly. Jua kept sniffling. Yuji handed her the last of her wet wipes and asked, "Where did you last see your mom?"

"Near a bench around the square."

"Let's go and see. That's where my parents were before they disappeared, too. I think they got so wrapped up in their argument that they forgot about me."

"Forgot about you?"

"Yeah, they do that once in a while. My mom and dad are like little kids, so I have to take care of them."

"I hope my mom just forgot, too. But there's no way she did."

"Yes, there is!" Yuji said, glaring at Jua. Jua's words, about how there was no way her mom had forgotten about her, annoyed her. *She's the one who's been abandoned,* Yuji thought, sulking inside. Blinking back her tears, Jua said she was sorry. She looked like she had no idea what she should be sorry for.

"Come on, we need to hurry. It'll be scary after the sun goes down," Yuji said.

"Right," Jua said in reply.

Together, Yuji and Jua looked all around the square. They even went to where the Hamster Wheel was—which Yuji didn't want to do—but there was no one there either. Yuji felt exhausted. As she had left the Lost Children Center, she had thought that she would find her parents soon. Her face clouded over. Then suddenly, Jua asked her a question, as if she had an idea in mind.

"How did you get here?"

"Me? I came by car."

"I came on a shuttle bus so it won't work for me, but why don't we go check the parking lot since you came by car?" Jua asked.

She was blinking her eyes with such an innocent look on her face that Yuji felt a prick of annoyance and had to look away. She had actually already thought of the parking lot. But it was probably a waste of time—if the car wasn't in the parking lot, that meant her parents had left without her. That was impossible. Putting aside her uneasy feelings, Yuji shook her head. Then after catching her breath she said, "We don't need to go to the parking lot because they're still in the park for sure."

"But ..."

"Once you leave, you can't come back inside. Do you want me to leave you behind here?"

"No, but ..."

Yuji pulled Jua by the wrist. Jua followed without resistance, like a paper doll. Again, they began looking everywhere in the park. Jua didn't bring up the parking lot again.

It was almost evening already. The heat had lifted somewhat, but the girls were hungry. Yuji and Jua, tired and worn out, sat side by side on a bench. As they sat there and watched other people, they realized that everyone else in the park looked like they were having a good time. They thought it was unfair that only the two of them had to go through all these troubles. At that moment, Yuji spotted a face she recognized. It was the face of the man who had given her the jelly. He was handing out a packet of jelly to a couple in front of the carousel. His raspy voice made its way through the noise to Yuji's ears.

"How long have you been together? You'll never split up if you share this jelly," he was saying.

The guy smiled without much of a reaction, but the girl broke into giggles. Yuji recalled the jelly the man had given her. *So he just says that to everyone,* she thought.

She hadn't really put her hopes in the jelly, but she still felt disappointed somehow. She felt weak. She had gone around busily without eating anything since that skimpy lunch, and now her stomach was growling loudly. It seemed Jua wasn't any better off. Yuji pulled out the crumpled packet of jelly from her backpack and tore it open. A sweet and sour smell rose to her nose.

"Here, have some of this," she said to Jua.

"Is that jelly? I love jelly!" Jua said, reaching into the packet and taking a handful of jelly before Yuji had even had any. Grains of crystal clear sugar fell like snow from her hands. The jelly, light pink in color, looked like it would taste like strawberries. Jua was about to put a couple of pieces into her mouth but then stopped to smell them.

"They smell really funny," she said.

"They do?" Yuji asked and reached into the packet herself. She grabbed a handful, and as she raised her head, she noticed a stranger. The woman, wearing a blue dress, was walking towards them with urgency.

The woman cried out, "Jua, is that you?"

Yuji froze and stared at the woman as she came toward them with bigger and bigger strides. Jua, oblivious to what was going on, was still examining the jelly and swinging her feet. The woman, now right in front of them, stood before Jua, whose head was bowed. Yuji took a look at the woman's profile. She had red-rimmed eyes like Jua had after crying tons. The two looked almost ridiculously alike. Noticing the long shadow over her, Jua finally lifted her head. Her face wrinkled up like a boiled dumpling left out for too long. Face to face with the woman, she began bawling, even louder than she had at the Lost Children Center.

"Mom! I hate you!" she screamed.

The woman quickly took Jua into her arms. She kept saying that she was sorry as she stroked Jua's disheveled hair over and over again. Yuji stared at them, the thought of jelly gone from her mind. She felt as if she was watching a scene from the soap opera that her grandmother watched religiously every weekend. She wasn't sure how she should react, but she sure didn't feel too happy for Jua. Yuji took a slow look around, but her parents were still nowhere to be seen.

Yuji got to her feet. The ground was scattered with pieces of jelly that had fallen from Jua's hand. Yuji stared at her own hands, which had nothing to hold on to, and the stupid packet of jelly. In irritation she crumpled up the packet that still had jelly inside.

A faint crying sound pierced her ears. Yuji looked around. A cat jumped out from under the bench she had been sitting on and looked intently at her. The black and white of the cat's coat seemed familiar somehow, then she realized that it was Dream Kitty, the mascot of New Seoul Park. Good luck was supposed to come to you all day if you ran into Dream Kitty at the park, but Yuji's situation was far from lucky. Perhaps all the luck had gone to Jua, who had found her mom.

"Good luck, my foot!" Yuji muttered to herself.

The cat's yellow eyes were gleaming brightly. Yuji was seething deep inside with a feeling she couldn't describe. She picked up a piece of jelly from the ground and threw it at the cat. The cat, of course, didn't eat the jelly. Yuji glared at the cat. She couldn't let herself glare at Jua—she would feel too small and petty.

The cat came near Yuji's feet. Yuji stomped her feet in irritation. Unruffled, the cat kept hovering around her. The tearful reunion of Jua and her mom was still under way. Yuji crammed the crumpled packet of jelly back into her backpack.

Jua's mom took Jua and Yuji to a café nearby. It was the café where Yuji had had lunch with her parents. The interior was colorful and pretty, but the portions were too small compared to the price and the food didn't even taste good. After ordering an ice cream and a smoothie, Jua's mom came to the table and sat down. Sitting across from her, Yuji realized that her eyes and mouth looked exactly like Jua's, which kind of spooked her. Her stomach churned as she watched the two, sitting face to face. Feelings she couldn't control were running rampant inside her. Unable to bring herself to smile, Yuji just stared at a corner of the table.

"I'm going to the restroom, so you wait here," Jua's mom said.

"No, I'm coming with you," Jua said. Having bawled her eyes out, she was now set on acting like a child.

As her mom got to her feet, Jua did the same and followed her to the bathroom. She was like a baby chick following its mother. Yuji sat there, picking at the ice cream in front of her with a plastic spoon.

The ice cream was strawberry-flavored, her favorite, but she couldn't seem to taste anything. She felt cold and empty inside, maybe because of the air conditioner just across from her. Yuji hung her head and fiddled with the backpack on her knees. She opened the zipper and saw the shiny crumpled packet of jelly. She recalled what the man had said when he had given her the packet:

"They will never split up."

But how? Was it magic jelly or something? But having seen the way he talked to the couple earlier, Yuji thought that he was probably just trying to market the jelly. She placed the crumpled packet on the table. The jelly looked like ordinary junk food. She opened the packet and reached inside. It was sticky, the sugar having melted from the heat. Yuji pulled out the first piece her fingers touched and took a glance around. No one in the café was paying any attention to her.

Yuji pulled Jua's smoothie toward her and dropped the jelly into the cup. The smoothie, made from strawberries, was thick and close in color to the jelly. One piece of jelly would go without being noticed. It would sink to the bottom of the cup, and Jua would chew and swallow the jelly along with the pieces of fruit in the smoothie. If not, well, too bad.

The jelly, though, rose to the surface, probably because it was too light. Just then, the restroom door opened and Jua came out. Yuji hastily stirred the smoothie with the straw to try and make the jelly sink. As she did, the jelly spread out like liquid and melted into the smoothie like magic.

What just happened? Yuji wondered, frozen with the straw in her hand.

Jua's mom had also come back and asked her in a kind voice, "Would you like a smoothie, too?"

"No, thank you," Yuji replied, quickly putting down the straw. Then she hurriedly stuffed the half-melted ice cream into her mouth. It didn't taste like anything. Her heart was beating fast. Jua's mom must have been thirsty because she sat and gulped down the smoothie Yuji had stirred up. Jua reached for the cup too, saying she wanted some as well. Jua ended up drinking more than half of the smoothie. Her heart thumping like crazy, Yuji watched them finish the drink without a word.

"Yuji, right? Do you remember your address?" Jua's mom asked.

"It's P Apartments, complex number two, number 405 …"

"Do you remember which block it is? When did you last see your parents?"

Jua's mom tried to find Yuji's address by searching for the location on her cell phone. Then as the sun began to set, she got to her feet and said, "Your parents could have gone to the Lost Children Center after you left. Let's take one last look, then go to the police station."

Yuji nodded her head. The theme park took on a mysterious color under the sunset. The people, probably waiting for the night parade, looked calmer than they had during the day. Dream Teddy, who had been dancing incessantly like a broken robot, was nowhere to be seen. Feeling anxious, Yuji kept her eyes fixed on Jua and her mom. There was no sign of even the slightest bit of change.

Jua didn't want to be away from her mom's side, not for an instant. Jua's mom was being just as dramatic—she kept Jua at her side, caressing her face and taking her into her arms again and again. Yuji couldn't understand. In her eyes, Jua was a baby, so immature compared to herself. All she knew how to do by herself was cry. She was childish and dumb.

So why was Jua's mom looking at her with such infinite love in her eyes? Yuji had never seen her parents look at her that way. Not even once. Yuji clenched her fists in her pocket. She bit the inside of her mouth. It stung and she tasted blood, but she was able to keep the tears from welling up in her eyes.

Even when the sun had almost set and hung behind the mountain peaks, no change came over Jua and her mom. The man had just been trying to promote jelly after all. Yuji heaved a long sigh. She hadn't expected a dramatic change, but she couldn't help feeling a bit disappointed. At the same time, though, she felt a little relieved.

Yuji walked, following the long shadows ahead of her and looking at the patterned tiles on the ground. Jua and her mom had been walking ahead but came to a sudden stop. Yuji raised her head and looked at them. Jua, walking happily along just a moment ago, suddenly grasped her throat and fell to the ground.

"What's wrong, Jua?" Jua's mom asked in alarm.

Jua's face was growing redder by the second. There was something wrong with her breathing, as if she had a fish bone stuck in her throat. Jua's mom sat on the ground, thumping her on the back. Her hands shook uncontrollably as she pulled out her cell phone. Yuji swallowed hard. Her heart was pounding like a drum.

Blargh!

Jua threw up. A clear pink slime oozed out of her mouth as she lay on her side. Jua's mom dropped her phone. She frantically started grabbing onto passersby and screaming for help. One by one, people came to a stop. Someone went to get a park employee. The employee, grasping the situation, promptly called 911.

Jua, sprawled out on the ground, reached her arms toward her mom. Her mom picked her up and carried her on her back. Then gently rocking her little girl, she mumbled quietly to comfort her.

"It's all right, it's all right."

It seemed that she was trying to tell herself that as well. Jua appeared to have calmed down a bit and was no longer squirming around. Her back rose and fell in big heaving breaths as she clung to her mom's back. Her flimsy short-sleeved top was drenched in sweat.

Something was odd. Yuji took a closer look at Jua's back. The damp fabric of her shirt had a strange sheen to it. It looked sticky, not wet, as if it had syrup on it. Goosebumps rose on Yuji's neck. An intensely sweet smell suddenly attacked her. Yuji held her nose. She was familiar with this pungent smell, this sweet and sour smell that stung her nose and made her sneeze.

Even though she was holding her nose, it still itched inside, causing Yuji to sneeze a couple of times. It seemed that others had gotten a whiff of the strange smell, too; people were sneezing everywhere. While taking a deep breath, Yuji realized what the smell was. It had the same smell as the jelly in her backpack.

"I can't reach 911—does anyone have a phone that works?"

The employee, who should have talked to 911 by now, shouted with an urgent look on her face and a hand in the air. People who had been watching began to pull out their phones and make calls. Then their faces fell. The murmurs grew louder. Yuji couldn't understand what was going on. Everyone was raising their arms high in order to try and get a signal on their phones. But there was no service.

"What's going on?"

The phones had all shut down, the screens black. Shaken with anxiety, everyone started asking questions. Yuji thought she caught a glimpse of the jelly vendor in the crowd, but when she rubbed her eyes and opened them again, she didn't see anyone who looked even remotely like him.

Things became increasingly chaotic. People were more upset that their phones didn't have a signal than by the state Jua was in. Feeling nervous, Yuji kept her eyes on Jua and her mom. Jua's face was buried in her mom's shoulder—she must have fallen asleep. Holding Jua's hand tight, Jua's mom let out a deep breath. Having calmed down a bit, she looked around for Yuji.

Standing in the crowd, Yuji met her eyes. Yuji watched as Jua's mom came toward her. Her face buried in her mom's shoulder, Jua showed no signs of moving.

"You must be shocked, too. I don't think I can come with you to the police station. Let's go talk to that employee over there," Jua's mom said with difficulty.

The words didn't register. Her body stiff as stone and her eyes unblinking, Yuji stared at Jua's mom as she talked. There was something wrong with her complexion. Her face had been as white as a sheet just a moment ago; now it was crimson red. Only when Yuji realized that she wasn't dreaming did she blink her eyes. The strangely flushed face of Jua's mom turned a deeper and deeper red. She looked just like Jua before she had passed out. Yuji slowly backed away.

"What ... what's wrong?" Jua's mom asked, looking puzzled,

as Yuji backed away with a frightened look on her face. Then Jua's mom, who had been standing still, suddenly convulsed.

Blargh! Blargh!

Dark red blood spilled out of her mouth. Mingled with the blood was what looked like half-digested pink phlegm. The people around them all screamed at once. Jua's mom covered her mouth with her hands. Her body shook violently back and forth a couple of times, as though some alien creature was about to come ripping out of her. At that moment, Jua, still on her mom's back, shouted something.

"Ahm, I-ahdi-ee-elting!"

"What? What did you say, Jua?" her mom asked, again and again, but Jua wasn't able to answer clearly. Her words were blurred, as though her tongue had dissolved. Yuji's face grew pale amid the commotion. Yuji had understood what Jua was trying to say.

Mom, my body is melting. That was what Jua was saying.

No paramedics were on their way. Not a single phone was working. Everywhere it reeked of a sweet, sickening smell. Something strange was happening. Yuji stood fixed to her spot among the crowd, watching and taking in all that was happening. Her hands, clenched into fists, were clutching the shoulder straps of her backpack. "*They will never split up.*" Again, the man's words rang in her mind. It was an awakening of sorts. Yuji was overcome by the feeling that she knew what was about to unfold.

"Let's put the girl down first. You don't look very well yourself—let's get you some first aid," someone in the crowd said, stepping forward. It seemed that he was in the medical profession; he sounded quite decisive. But even before he had finished speaking, Jua's mom grasped the hem of his shirt and clung to him. Her face was closer to pink now, and there was a bloodstain around her mouth as well as the mysterious pink liquid. She said, almost sobbing, "I can't get her off of me …."

Only then did Yuji, and everyone around her, realize that there was something abnormal about the way the woman and her daughter were positioned. Jua's mom was covering her mouth with one hand and clinging to the man with the other. And yet Jua stayed on her back, not slipping or falling off. Yuji's eyes widened. Jua's little arms, wrapped around her mom's neck, began to dribble down like sticky caramel syrup.

Yuji recalled the French toast she had once had with her mom at a dessert shop. Sticky syrup and fruit jam had come trickling out when she had stuck her fork into the toast. Yuji blinked her eyes. Was everything she was seeing real? Or was it just a dream? Jua's arms, legs, shoulders, and head were trickling down like the syrup from her memory.

Jua, sticky now, soon began to spread over her mom's body, which was supporting her. It seemed that nothing could pull them apart, like caramel in a glass jar that had not been taken out all summer. Then a bizarre change came over Jua's mom as well. Her skin took on a glow, and her knees went soft. She couldn't stand properly, as if her body had no joints.

Yuji couldn't move, like someone was holding her by the ankles. She stared at how Jua and her mom were stuck together. Screaming, the passerby took Jua's mom's hand off his wrist, and her fingers stretched out, just like when jelly melts in the mouth. Jua's mom shrieked. People scattered away, screeching.

The sound of screaming, which had been coming from the roller coaster in the distance, was now coming from nearby.

The harder Jua's mom tried to get Jua off her, the more entangled they became. The two—now one—fell to the ground. Surrendering to their fate, they began to melt away together. Their faces, shoulders, arms, legs, and hands dissolved into one big lump. As the lump slowly melted, what used to be Jua's face squirmed. The round lump spun calmly around, as though it was taking a look at its surroundings. The drifting head then faced Yuji, and its creepy white eyeballs, not yet melted, locked onto her face.

Jua blinked her eyes slowly, then went completely limp. All that was left now was sticky, pink jelly and her clothes. The blue dress Jua's mom had been wearing took on a peculiar hue—neither blue nor pink—having merged with the syrupy pink liquid.

There was no one left around Yuji. With great difficulty, she finally managed to move her legs. She took a step back, then another. The lump of jelly that had once been an affectionate mother and her daughter had spread out wide, leaving behind only what they had been wearing and carrying.

"It's all because of that jelly …" Yuji mumbled.

Jua's last look haunted her. She felt as if Jua was blaming her. No, she was certain—Jua knew everything. Yuji turned around and ran, shutting her eyes tight. With every step she took, she sensed how unbelievably slimy the ground was.

Had Jua seen her put the jelly in the smoothie? Did she know everything? It seemed impossible but also possible at the same time. Yuji ran until she was out of breath and couldn't run anymore. When she finally got a hold of herself, she found that she

The New Seoul Park Jelly Massacre

was standing in front of the restroom. She took out the packet of jelly from her backpack and went into the restroom. Her hands were slippery and the backpack fell onto the dirty floor, but she didn't care.

"I have to get rid of this," she mumbled urgently. Her feet stepped onto something sticky. Yuji looked down at her feet. It was the clear pink jelly again. She thought that the melted mother and daughter had followed her. Screaming, Yuji sank to the floor. *Splash!* Her buttocks got wet in the pool of jelly and water.

Looking more closely, she realized that it wasn't Jua and her mother. Though faint, it had the form of a man and a woman. They were still in the process of melting. They looked like a couple and were hugging each other tight. Or rather, it seemed that one had been struggling to push the other away, and then they had ended up becoming stuck together. Unlike the man with the crumbled features, the woman, whose face was still mostly intact, looked quite peaceful and happy.

The woman's face looked curiously familiar. Searching her memory, Yuji realized that it was the couple who had gotten a packet of jelly from the man. She flung her packet of jelly, which she had been holding tightly in her hand, far away. The long oval pieces of jelly scattered away, bouncing off the restroom floor. Yuji jerked back, still on her buttocks, screaming. Her ears were numb. She couldn't, for some reason, hear her own voice. She tried screaming louder, but she still couldn't hear anything. She got to her feet and ran out of the restroom. Soon she learned why she couldn't hear herself screaming; everyone in the theme park was screaming.

What she saw was people turning into jelly, and people who

had already turned into jelly, tangled together all over the place. Yuji stood in a daze. The scene somehow looked like a parade presented by the theme park. The sweet, pungent smell made her feel sick. She was dizzy. Yuji thought of her parents in the midst of all the chaos. Where could they be? Had they already turned into jelly somewhere in the park?

Pink jelly was taking over the colorful paving blocks. Staring at the people melting away, Yuji imagined that the theme park was a miniature toy belonging to some gigantic organism. Although before they had just silently watched the toy, they were now sick of it and had decided that the toy should serve another purpose and had filled it with something sticky. Yuji felt as though she were standing alone, staring blankly around her, in a glass jar full of jam. Like those fixed figurines in snow globes.

Slimy liquid from a lump somewhere had reached Yuji's feet. Yuji kicked again and again at the slime, which no longer bore the shape of a human. Little drops of jelly splattered onto her pants.

Only one thought stood clear in the chaos of her mind: she had to find her mom and dad in this strange theme park. *What if they've turned into human jelly, too, while looking for me?* As her imagination went wild, Yuji shook her head. As long as she got herself out of this glass jar of a theme park, she would be able to escape this nightmare. She was a mature, perfect child, so she could find them. She was the only one who could take care of her parents. At that moment, a raspy voice, which she didn't recognize but felt that she had heard before, interrupted her thoughts. Yuji looked straight ahead.

The New Seoul Park Jelly Massacre

"Do you think your parents are here?" the voice asked.

It was the man who had given her the jelly. He had come out of nowhere. She was standing face to face with him, but she couldn't discern the features of his face. Yuji rubbed her eyes. It was no use. His face was still shrouded in darkness, his voice was as shady and damp as a cave, and his features were blurred. Yuji backed away. The lump of jelly she had just kicked splashed up on her. She could feel little pieces of bones, not yet completely melted, under her feet. The man opened his mouth although she couldn't see it. She imagined a black hole opening and closing. The voice came from inside her head.

"They're not here. Where could they be, then?" said the voice.

"No," Yuji replied.

Let's go to the parking lot, let's go see if the car's there. This time it was Jua who had whispered in her ear. Yuji covered her ears.

"They're home. They probably went to sleep, forgetting all about you."

"That's not true!"

The man grinned, his mouth stretching from ear to ear. The grotesque smile was the only part of his blurred face that she could see clearly.

"You don't believe me?" the man asked, reaching out a hand. Yuji stared at the tip of the dark hand coming towards her. She was frozen to her spot.

"Let me take you home, then."

You're going to the parking lot; you've been abandoned; I've melted away, but at least I'm with my mom; but not you; you're alone. Jua whispered in a singsong voice. Yuji blacked out.

The Survivor

Dream Teddy, the mascot of New Seoul Park, had short brown fur. Stars always shone in his black eyes. People often mistook him for a mouse because his ears were a bit too wide for a bear and because he had a protruding mouth. In the early days of the park, there had been some disputes as to the identity of the mascot, as some people argued that it was an imitation of a character from a famous theme park abroad. But in any case, thanks to the park's brazen strategy, Dream Teddy managed to become the mascot of New Seoul Park. An icon of fun, he was the first thing people saw in the main square upon entering.

Dream Teddy, always looking happy and innocent, was in charge of handing out balloons to children. He danced when children asked him to dance and struck a pose when they wanted to take pictures with him. Some children were mean to him, thinking he wouldn't fight back. At that very moment, a kid standing in front of Dream Teddy was ruthlessly stabbing him in the shoulder with a toy knife, which he had either brought from home or bought at a shop.

The kid snickered, watching Dream Teddy as he clutched his

shaking head. Soon the kid's parents came toward them from a distance with churros in their hands, and the kid, having let go of the balloon that Dream Teddy had given him, disappeared with sugar all over his mouth. Dream Teddy stood still in his spot. He was supposed to be dancing at that moment, going round and round. But the only thing that was going round and round was his mind. He didn't want to move a finger.

"Fuck …."

Dream Teddy looked as happy and innocent as ever as he spat out the word under his breath. He had no choice, as looking happy and innocent was his job.

Sajun, who had to be Dream Teddy from 10 a.m. to 3 p.m., readjusted the bear head that had shifted a little to the side. The kid's attack hadn't physically hurt him. Things like that happened all the time. Kids that age were rowdy, and he had been through worse. But on a day as hot as this, any little thing could provoke anger. On top of that, the bear head was humid and stank. He couldn't even begin to describe how unpleasant it felt.

The sound of the kid snickering on top of all that was like a very sharp knife, a real knife heated in fire, scorching his insides.

The New Seoul Park theme song came to an end, then started over from the beginning. Sajun, too, returned to his designated spot. Concealing his anger, he began to dance again. He spread out his arms, jumped on one foot and then the other, and twirled around and around. He saw kids flocking from a distance like a pack of beasts. He began to mumble something, sounding glum. You couldn't make out the words unless you put your ear right up against Dream Teddy's head.

The New Seoul Park Jelly Massacre

"My monthly pay of 180, plus overtime pay for the extra parade, minus ten for phone and internet, twenty for food, and twenty-five for living expenses; so I should have about x left. Add that to the money in my account, and I should have x. How much would I have in a year if I put that much into a monthly installment savings account? And how much more would I need to get a place in Seoul …"

Sajun was constantly doing these calculations. The numbers were like his own theme song that brought him peace of mind. On the pretext that he couldn't really do the math in his head, he rounded off the numbers—he rounded up for his income and rounded down for his expenses. Adding and subtracting hypothetical numbers again and again gave him satisfactory results. Repeating the numbers over and over again, Sajun danced to the New Seoul Park theme song. In the meantime, children had gathered around him, holding out their little hands for balloons. Dream Teddy smiled, looking happy and innocent.

*

Anxiously, Sajun counted his remaining meal tickets. He had ten left, but the end of the month was still weeks away. They only gave out thirty tickets a month for meals. People didn't live on just one meal a day—thirty was far from enough for all three meals a day. *Shouldn't they provide at least three meals a day to someone who lived in the dormitory, having come all the way from the provinces to work at the park?* True, a high proportion of the staff were students who had applied for the job just for the experience and fun, but some people had to work for a living.

He might have to start paying for his meals in the coming weeks. Sajun headed to his room, turning down his co-workers who wanted to order in some late-night food. His entire body ached after hours of standing in the scorching sun. He had a hard time just lifting his arm to open the door; he felt like he could go to sleep standing if there was something he could lean on. "Let's wash up and go to bed," he mumbled and turned on the light. The bluish light of the fluorescent bulb revealed the mess that was his room.

Sajun felt irritated to the point of exasperation. He had cleaned the room just the weekend before, but it was now so messy that there was no space to walk around. A musty smell of mold and sweat mixed together filled the room, and dirty laundry was scattered all over the floor. That wasn't all. There was something else that really got to him, the rough crumbs that grated against the soles of his feet with each step he took. It was sugar from all kinds of candy, including jelly. The parade of sugar, which began at the front door, continued up to his roommate's bunk. Narrowing his eyes, Sajun noticed that there was white powder even on the blanket. Annoyed, he walked over and pushed the covers aside. Sure enough, there was a huge bag of jelly on the bed.

The drowsiness that had been about to engulf Sajun flowed away like a low tide. He pulled out a garbage bag from the cabinet and threw whatever his hands came across on the floor into the bag. He had asked nicely, more than a few times. Yeongdu, his roommate, never paid attention to what anyone said. Sajun had said many times that they should practice common courtesy since they were living together. Yeongdu had nodded along, but nothing ever changed. As a result the double room, which should have been pleasant enough, was always full of garbage and infested with bugs because of the sugar and bits of snacks Yeongdu scattered everywhere. Sajun even had an ant crawl into his mouth once while he was lying down. He had now given up trying to talk to Yeongdu.

He couldn't, however, leave the room messy. Having stuffed everything he found on the floor into the garbage bag, Sajun straightened his back and walked over to his roommate's bed. A laptop computer—Yeongdu's prized possession—was sitting in a corner, emitting a bluish light. On the screen was probably the online community site which Yeongdu spent his time on all night. Yeongdu only got animated when he was talking about what a big shot he was in the online world. But Sajun had no interest whatsoever in which online community he participated in, and whenever Yeongdu got excited and raved on about himself, Sajun quietly put in his earphones. His guess was that it was probably an 18+ website for pathetic losers who thought sharing dirty jokes made them look cool, or a shady website for those who were obsessed with cartoon characters to the point of doting on them as if they were real.

On the laptop screen was a bizarre image of an ancient engraving, under which flashed a password window. The engraving showed what looked like the devil and people dancing below in a circle, with a huge cauldron at the center. A gleaming human wrist was protruding from the seething cauldron. It was sickening. Frowning, Sajun turned his head away.

He then took out the miniature vacuum cleaner from under the desk and began to suck up all the sugar on the floor.

Yeongdu didn't show up while Sajun was cleaning; he was probably having dinner. He wouldn't have been much help anyway, but Sajun couldn't help feeling that it was unfair for him to do all the cleaning.

He was vacuuming under Yeongdu's desk and massaging his aching back when he noticed something strange. It was a paper box, the corners tattered from too much handling. On the outside, it looked like a gift box for cookies. Without really thinking about it, Sajun picked up the box. The box opened easily. A sweet smell entered his nose, along with the smell of damp paper.

"What is this?" Sajun wondered aloud.

The sheets of faded yellow paper were packed with mysterious patterns and cryptic signs—he couldn't even tell if they were pictures or words. He turned the pages, but they all looked alike. He couldn't even begin to guess what they were for, but the longer he looked at them, the more they creeped him out.

Sajun heard the door open behind him. He turned his head and looked at the door. Yeongdu was standing there with a steaming cup of instant noodles. His sunken eyes were looking at Sajun's hands—at the paper in Sajun's hands, to be precise. Hastily closing the box, Sajun said, "Oh, hey."

"Why are you going through my stuff?"

Yeongdu's sharp screech pierced his ears. Yeongdu glared at him, his bloodshot eyes full of spite. Sajun was flabbergasted. The guy was mad at him for opening some stupid box, when he had slaved away cleaning up all the mess that the guy had made. Sajun shook the box violently on purpose. The box was so flimsy and light that he felt like it would vanish any minute.

The New Seoul Park Jelly Massacre

"What is this, anyway?" he asked.

"Don't touch it!" Yeongdu shouted, lunging at him. It was incredible that he had so much strength in that scrawny body of his. Yeongdu's long fingernails scratched at Sajun's arm. A sharp pain shot through his body. Yeongdu, having snatched the box away in an instant, cradled it in his arms and glared at Sajun. Bewildered, Sajun stared at Yeongdu, then at the scratches on his arm. Steam rose from the spilled noodles on the floor. The irritation flaring up inside Sajun overwhelmed him, draining him of energy. Sajun pointed to the mess on the floor and said, "Whatever. Why don't you just clean that up."

Yeongdu said nothing in reply. "Who cares," Sajun muttered under his breath as he climbed onto his bunk. Soon, he could hear the sound of Yeongdu slowly cleaning the floor. Sajun pulled the covers over his head. Only when some time had passed and the lights were completely turned off did he pull down the covers.

Though he was exhausted, Sajun was having trouble falling asleep. This time, it was the sound of Yeongdu typing furiously in the lower bunk. Now that he was aware of the sound, it was impossible for him to ignore it and go to sleep. Yeongdu was always like this. Night after night, he would type away, grating on Sajun's nerves. The tapping sound created by Yeongdu's fingers and the keyboard assailed his eardrums. Sajun pulled the blanket back over his head. He felt a bit stifled, but at least the sound faded somewhat. Quietly, he began to chant his spell.

"How much do I have left in my bank account? I have 180 coming in for my monthly pay, plus overtime pay, minus ten for phone and internet, and twenty for food. Twenty for food … the meal tickets are nowhere near enough. And let's say thirty for expenses, so I should have about x left. Add that to the money in my account, and I should have about x. I have five meal tickets left, so if I use one a day for five days …"

Peace settled in his heart after a little while. The peace would be shattered once he woke up in the morning, but it was all the more precious for that reason. Not even the sound of typing from the lower bunk could disturb his peace. Sajun relaxed, and closed his eyes.

How had Yeongdu ended up the way he was? What did he do every night on his laptop? Was it really possible for someone like him to become a celebrity in the online world? Then how much—or how little—of what was said there could actually be believed? Sajun tried to relieve the stress that came from his inconsiderate roommate by sympathizing with the pathetic guy, but if this stress was something that could be relieved just like that, things would never have come to this.

Just before he drifted off to sleep, Sajun recalled the rumor he had heard when he had first started working at the park. The rumor that Yeongdu had a weird obsession.

*

It was thanks to that rumor that Sajun had been able to get the double room. No one had volunteered to share a room with Yeongdu for months. Seeing the manager's dilemma that they couldn't let the space go unused, Sajun had volunteered without hesitation. All the other rooms in the dormitory were for four people. Sajun was tired of living with a lot of people in one room. The manager was happy that he volunteered, but for some reason, those who had started working at the park around the same time as Yeongdu had looked at him with concern. It was only after he had moved in all his belongings that Sajun learned of the rumor.

The manager had told the story during the dinner get-together for the new recruits. The attraction division overflowed with volunteers, but the souvenir shop was always in need of a merchandiser. As a place where money came and went, there were a lot of difficult customers, and most of the people who came to work at the park didn't want a sales position—that was, after all, a job that could be found easily outside of the park. So the manager had put Yeongdu in the position when he had volunteered, without thinking about it too much.

Strange things began to happen, though, after Yeongdu began working there. The souvenir shop sold jelly—which didn't sell very quickly—out of a clear acrylic container. First, the shop began to run out of jelly twice as fast, but the sales remained the same. It meant that someone was pocketing the jelly. But no one took the problem seriously at the time; it was just jelly, not money, after all.

That wasn't all. A rumor began to go around that the dormitory building was cursed. Many of the park employees said that they had seen or heard something while going to the bathroom at night. The building was infested with bugs, too many even for summer, and reeked of something rotting on rainy days. People often found ants crawling on their skin while sleeping, and the humidity wouldn't drop even with the air conditioning on all day. In the end, on the hottest day of the summer, the park hired a disinfection company.

"What's this door?" asked a man from the company. He had been inspecting the building and was now pointing to a storage room at the end of the third-floor corridor. Kept in the storage room were things that former employees had lost or left behind; no one used it anymore, and it was left as it was. The man sniffed at the door, saying he suspected the storage room to be the cause.

"A sudden increase in bugs means that they've built a nest for themselves. Haven't you heard stories of people who noticed that there were a lot of bees in the house all of a sudden, then after tearing down a wall for remodeling, found a beehive inside? Though they couldn't tell how on earth the bees had built a hive in cement. Stories like that. Anyway, it means that there has to be a place in this building occupied by bugs."

There was no key to the storage. The manager asked the office, but all they got in reply was that the key was long lost. So, they searched the entire building except the storage room but found nothing else that could be the cause of the bugs. Therefore, to open the storage room, the only place that hadn't been searched, a locksmith was brought in. The locksmith got the door open by removing the entire doorknob. The moment the door opened, everyone held their nose.

Recalling the smell, the manager described it as "a sweet, rotten smell." He said that the musty odor, so pungent that he was afraid to breathe, had a hint of a very sweet, fruity smell to it. Sajun couldn't even imagine it. He knew what a rotten smell was, but what on earth was a sweet, rotten smell? Anyway, the mystery was solved; the countless pieces of jelly that had vanished from the souvenir shop was behind the smell.

The New Seoul Park Jelly Massacre

Inside the storage was a huge pile of jelly. The tremendous amount of jelly had turned into one big lump and was melting in the storage room, which was as hot as a sauna due to the sweltering heat of summer. The jelly, stacked in layers and sticking together at random, looked like a bizarre sculpture. Recalling the scene, the manager made a face and said, "It was a sticky, pink hell. A sticky hell for ants."

Sajun thought it was a very poor description, considering the serious look on the manager's face.

Even with the disinfection process under way, the ants marched in ceaselessly. The bugs that came, lured by the sweet smell, got caught in the sticky lump and died there. The traces of these bugs looked like black mold, scattered here and there on the pink lump.

The manager went to see Yeongdu straight away. There was plenty of evidence. The day before, the manager had asked Yeongdu to clean up after his shift, while pretending he was leaving early, and found afterwards that a good amount of jelly had clearly gone missing. The manager went to the double room that Yeongdu had to himself after his roommate quit and banged on the door so hard that it seemed it would break. Yeongdu finally opened the door after a while. He didn't even ask what it was all about, and the manager shoved him aside and entered the room.

The walls were covered with patterns drawn in an unidentifiable red liquid. On the floor was the drawing of a big star, with jelly at every tip: star-shaped jelly, bean-shaped jelly, shark-shaped jelly, fried-egg-shaped jelly. Yeongdu was mumbling these same words over and over again like a lunatic, "I need the book, I failed because I don't have the book. If only I had the book …"

"What's all this?" the manager asked Yeongdu, forcing a laugh.

Yeongdu replied, as though it was the most obvious thing in the world, with the word, "Jelly."

That summer, a part-timer who worked as a mascot died from the intense heat. Yeongdu managed not to get fired and was instead transferred to the character division where Sajun currently worked. This had been possible because at the time, the park employees were under the direct supervision of the park management committee, without the intervention of an affiliate company.

When he had first heard the rumor, Sajun hadn't thought much of it. The guy hadn't harmed anyone after all; he was just crazy about jelly and had done something weird with it. What mattered more to Sajun was having personal space in a room that had as few people as possible. He could easily ignore a rumor like that if it was for the sake of getting out of this awful dormitory in a mountain village and getting a decent place in Seoul.

*

The next day, Sajun headed to the dormitory cafeteria in the basement with a meal ticket. Breakfast was a must if you were to wear a bulky mascot costume and shake your body to the music in this blistering heat. He was sitting in a corner of the cafeteria and stuffing his face when someone came and sat down across the table.

"Hi, it's been a while," the guy said. He was one of the people who had started working around the same time Sajun had; the two of them talked every now and then.

"Hi," Sajun replied in a low voice.

"It sucks to wear a mascot costume in this weather, doesn't it?" the guy said, taking a look around. Then he began to complain about the attraction division, where he worked. "It sucks for us, too. Why are there so many people when it's so hot?"

Sajun went on eating, quietly nodding in agreement. Unlike Sajun, who could barely make it through each day, the other people who had started working around the same time as him just wanted to earn some pocket money, or finance a trip, or have some fun working at a theme park. Sajun felt uncomfortable whenever they casually mentioned something about their everyday life. It wasn't that they had done anything wrong; he just didn't want to be around them.

The same went for the guy sitting across from him. "*I'm going on a trip around Europe after the break. My parents said they'd pay for it, but I couldn't have them do that when I'm old enough to get a job and work for what I want.*" Sajun remembered every word of what he had said at the orientation though the guy himself probably didn't.

Sajun, suffering from a sense of inferiority, was the only one who didn't like him though. The guy was friendly with everyone, and everyone liked him because he was outgoing and always had a smile on his face. He also knew everything that went on in the theme park. And he had some unexpected news for Sajun.

"Oh, guess what. You and Yeongdu are roommates, right? I heard something yesterday that blew my mind. He's the personnel manager's nephew! That's why he didn't get fired, even after doing something so weird. That's why you need someone backing you up in life. It's so unfair!"

Sajun stared at him, his chopsticks frozen in the air.

"How do you know?" he asked.

"Oh, it's just something I heard. Remember the fat guy with glasses who was at our interviews? That's his uncle. When I heard that, I did recall that they looked alike. Oh, hey, Gayeong, over here!"

The guy waved at his friends, and they gradually gathered around him. As they did, the guy, who had been quite chatty to Sajun, seemed to forget all about him. Feeling awkward, Sajun quickly finished his food and got to his feet. The guy said, "See you later," before waving his hand, but Sajun didn't respond. They wouldn't run into each other while working anyway.

Sajun got dressed in his costume and grabbed a handful of balloons as usual. A lot of people had come already even though it was still early, probably because it was the weekend. A little girl holding her mom's hand was hesitantly approaching from a distance. For someone who had come to a theme park, the girl didn't look very happy. Sajun held out a balloon for her. As she came up to him and reached out a hand, a group of kids rushed over.

The kids snatched away the balloons, every one of them brushing against Dream Teddy's tail and pants. Sajun was so busy dealing with them that when he finally gathered himself, he found that all the balloons were gone. The timid girl was still standing in front of him. Sajun shook off his hands in a gesture of apology, and the girl disappeared into the distance, pouting.

The girl's sad look weighed on his mind, but it wasn't something he could do anything about. He was distracted as it was

The New Seoul Park Jelly Massacre

because of what he had heard. He felt as though someone had dealt him a blow on the back of his head. He himself couldn't understand why he was so shocked.

People kept flocking in. Sajun was sweating buckets. He was so busy that he shouldn't have been able to think at all, but his mind seemed to have a will of its own. Even as he frantically shook his body to the music, what he had heard earlier kept going around in his mind.

So Yeongdu was the personnel manager's nephew. It was actually nothing compared to the outlandish rumor he had heard before. A personnel manager wasn't that important of a person, and there was nothing wrong with giving a relative a part-time position. So why was Sajun so upset? The more he thought about it, the more disturbed he felt.

"I have more than 180 coming in for my monthly pay, plus overtime pay, minus 9.5 for phone and internet and nineteen for food, and twenty-five for expenses, so I should have about x left. Add that to the money in my account, and I should have about x. Let's say I put that much into a monthly installment savings account, so to get a place in Seoul …"

Quietly, he chanted his little spell as he always did. He rounded up the numbers higher than usual and included a vacation bonus—which didn't even exist—but he still felt unsettled. In his mind, Yeongdu was no longer a recluse with no hope for the future, but a pampered rich boy with his uncle backing him.

It was so unfair. Here he was, trapped inside a fur suit in the middle of summer, without so much as a room to himself, and then there was Yeongdu, who lived a carefree life thanks to someone backing him up. Sajun felt a rush of anger inside him.

He wanted to fling off the bear head and hurl curses at the kids swarming around him, but reason—what little he had of it anyway—overcame that desire. Again, he began to quietly chant his little spell. He felt he would go crazy if he didn't.

The horde of kids finally left, and Sajun was able to catch his breath. He took a look at his surroundings in an effort to stop thinking about Yeongdu. The theme park was bustling as always. New Seoul Park, full of fun and dreams. Sajun had always thought that the place was too contrived. Even the fact that he, of all people, was the one inside Dream Teddy, the icon of fun, was unnatural. His gaze stopped on an employee standing on the other side of the carousel, selling jelly.

"Does he work here?" Sajun wondered to himself.

Yes, the employee was wearing the unfashionable yellow-green uniform, but Sajun had never seen him before. Was he a contract worker hired through an agency? Smiling good-naturedly, the employee handed out packets of jelly to passersby. Everyone—children and grown-ups alike—came and took a packet when they heard that they were free. The pink jelly in palm-sized packets was from a brand Sajun had never heard of.

"Promotion for a new product, I guess," Sajun muttered, and turned his head away.

The park did have PR people hired through an agency come in now and then. The New Seoul Park theme song started once again from the beginning. As Sajun began to dance, kids gathered around him. Dream Teddy turned around and around in his spot. He felt dizzy.

The New Seoul Park Jelly Massacre

The hands of the clock on the tower were already pointing to three o'clock. Soon his shift would be over and Yeongdu would take over. Sajun kept glancing at the clock tower through breaks in the crowd. It was considered good manners for the next shift employee to arrive ten minutes early. But Yeongdu wasn't there when it was almost three o'clock.

The anger that had been suppressed by his exhaustion reared its head again. Did being the personnel manager's nephew mean that one could be disrespectful like this? The ten or twenty minutes of extra work incurred by someone who didn't show up on time wasn't compensated by anyone.

The minute hand on the clock moved two minutes in no time. Sajun stopped moving and took off the bear head, revealing his sweaty, flushed face. A kid that had been coming closer to get a balloon flinched and pulled back. He turned around and ran back to his parents.

Sajun was sick of everything—everything about the theme park. *I wish it would all disappear*, he thought. Exasperated, he began to walk. People stared at him in curiosity as he tottered along, looking furious, with Dream Teddy's head under his arm. "What, what, what am I supposed to do?" he muttered to himself.

He had to get out of this ridiculous costume fast and have a word with Yeongdu. *So you're the personnel manager's nephew, are you? Makes things easy for you, huh?* He would snap, grabbing Yeongdu by his neck. Sajun realized that the sense of injustice he felt was like the jealousy he felt toward the people he worked with. The fact that he was feeling this way toward someone like Yeongdu crushed him more than anything else.

It wasn't surprising that Sajun, walking straight ahead in this state of great agitation, didn't notice a protruding paving block. Dream Teddy's bulging belly, of course, did not help either. Suddenly he fell on his face with a crash. The people around him all gasped in pity, and kids innocently laughed at him. Sajun did not want to get up. He wanted to just melt away.

When at last he managed to raise his head and prop himself up on his arms, someone reached out a helping hand. A familiar yellow-green uniform came into his view. It was the employee who had been handing out jelly to people. Sajun couldn't make out the man's features, hidden under a hat, even though he was face to face with the man. The bright sunlight shining down from behind the man cast a dark shadow on his face. Sajun stared at the hand in front of him. Normally, he would probably have taken the hand and said thank you. But he couldn't today. Actually, he didn't want to. He felt that the laughing kids were mocking him and that even the stray cats were insulting him as they meowed. The man standing in front of him was probably sneering at him, too, under that hat of his.

Ignoring the hand in front of him, Sajun got to his feet, though he had to struggle for quite a while to get Dream Teddy's puffy body up from the ground. He was about to walk away, ignoring the man in front of him, when the man held out a packet of jelly. It was the same jelly he had been handing out to people. Sajun was sick and tired of jelly. It made him think of the rumors about Yeongdu and the mess in the dorm room which nauseated him. He slapped down the packet and said in a cold voice, "You should worry about yourself—you're nothing but a short-term part-timer."

The packet of jelly fell to the ground. The man gazed at Sajun, his expression unchanging. Sajun felt rotten. He violently shoved past the man's shoulder and walked on. He felt the man's persistent gaze on him, but he didn't care. The man, seemingly indifferent to the insult inflicted on him, shouted in a cheerful voice, "Try some jelly! It's brand-new—you can't find it anywhere else!"

*

"Hey, do you know what time it is?" Sajun asked, knocking vigorously on the door.

He heard someone moving around inside.

"Have you been sleeping all this time?" Sajun asked in shock as the door opened.

Yeongdu wasn't ready for work at all. Sajun had had his problems with Yeongdu, but he hadn't imagined that he would be this irresponsible. He couldn't take it anymore. He took a deep breath, getting ready to spit out the words that had been pent up inside. Before he could even show his anger, though, Yeongdu interrupted in a higher voice than usual and said, "That's not important."

Sometimes feeling too much anger can make one laugh. Chuckling sarcastically, Sajun retorted by asking, "Oh, if work isn't important, then what …"

"I need your help, Sajun. Come with me," Yeongdu said, cutting him off.

Sajun was dumbfounded. Go with him where, in the middle of work hours? Was it something he could say because the personnel manager had his back? The thought was so absurd that it made him laugh again. He snapped at Yeongdu, telling him not to be ridiculous. Yeongdu pulled something out of his pocket. They were some crumpled-up fifty-thousand won bills. He tucked the bills into Sajun's pocket, saying, "Should be about 500,000 won total. You know that I've got no friends. This is really urgent. I have to go meet someone, and I think they might do something to me. That's why I want you to come with me. Nothing's going to happen though, probably not. So you just need to come with me and keep an eye on things. Don't worry about work. I'll get it all taken care of. And it's just 500,000 won for now, but I'll give you more when I get my pay. I mean it."

Reluctantly, Sajun stared at the yellow bills in his pocket. The moment he heard "500,000 won," the pent-up rage against Yeongdu had instantly subsided.

Sajun had the upper hand here. Standing with his head tilted and his arms folded, he looked down at Yeongdu. Yeongdu didn't seem to be joking. His eyes, gleaming more brightly than usual, looked somewhat creepy. Sajun did a quick calculation. The quiet chant now included a pleasant sum.

Fifty is what you get for at least three days of manual labor. So I'll have this fifty plus what's in my account. Fifty is the cost of a month's rent for a nice and comfortable studio apartment in Seoul ... wait, no, it should go toward the deposit. And then there's my monthly pay.

The thought of the windfall made him smile. His shift was over anyway, so he had nothing to lose. If the manager pressed him about Dream Teddy's absence, he could just tell him to ask Yeongdu about it. He even felt somewhat excited. Suppressing a smile, he pulled out the bills from his pocket and counted them. There were exactly ten bills.

"So all I have to do is come with you?"

Yeongdu quickly nodded, probably worried that Sajun would change his mind. Sajun wondered why Yeongdu was willing to go this far, but the specific amount of money he had in mind had a stronger pull over him at that moment. Still, he asked to make sure, "Are you sure it's not something dangerous? I don't have a good feeling about this."

"It's really no big deal. You don't even have to show yourself. You can just hide somewhere and take a video of us on your phone. Oh, is it more money you need?"

Yeongdu quickly ransacked his wardrobe, coming up with several ten-thousand won bills. This time, Sajun didn't even try to hide the look on his face and asked, "How much will you give me when you get your pay?"

"One third."

"Can you keep your word?"

Yeongdu nodded like a broken doll. Satisfied, Sajun took the bills and folded them up neatly before putting them in his pocket. He had received four extra ten-thousand won bills altogether. He added "plus four" to his chant.

They came to a plot of land outside the theme park, next to the mountain. The land had been meant for a water park that would have connected to the theme park, but some kind of real estate issue had kept it from being developed. A huge piece of slate prevented the general public from accessing the place, and the only entrance was a lattice door with a diamond pattern. On the door was a red sign that read AUTHORIZED PERSONNEL ONLY. Yeongdu opened the lock with a key, though there was no telling where he had gotten it from. Then he walked on, unruffled.

A weedy path led to a huge vacant lot and a small abandoned building. The lot was littered with broken ride parts and various construction materials. Among them was a bumper car modeled after Dream Teddy's head; the contrast between the super-bright eyes and the rusted body was eerie. It seemed that the discarded parts were from the rides that used to be in the park in its early days.

As Yeongdu had requested, Sajun turned on the video camera on his phone and hid inside the abandoned building. The long droopy vines and the tent would keep him hidden from view from the outside. Yeongdu was standing a little way off from the building. He looked tense, standing among the broken signboards and parts that looked like obstacles lying about. Sajun held his breath. He began to quietly chant his spell to ease his tension.

"My monthly pay, plus fifty-four or more; fifty-four or more ... how many hours would I have to work to earn that much?"

A soft smile rose to his lips. Everything was going to be fine. This was his lucky day. Elated, he went on chanting his little spell. He recalled the rumor about Yeongdu being the personnel manager's nephew, which triggered his sense of inferiority, but it was money, not pride, that put food on the table.

A car drove up the narrow path between the empty lot and the mountain. It was an imported luxury car that seemed to have no business being here in this deserted lot. Sajun's eyes widened. His curiosity reared its head at last, and he wondered who exactly Yeongdu was meeting. But there was no need to be impatient. He would find out soon enough if he just waited, phone in hand.

The New Seoul Park Jelly Massacre

A middle-aged woman, immaculate from head to toe, got out of the luxury car. Her short hair and dark gray suit made her look even more elegant. There was nothing flashy about her clothes, but even Sajun, who didn't know anything about luxury brands, could tell that everything she was wearing was expensive.

How on earth did Yeongdu get acquainted with someone like that? Was being the nephew of a personnel manager something significant after all? With these questions going around in his head, Sajun continued to quietly film the two. The woman approached Yeongdu. There was no hesitation in her stride. Standing face to face with the woman, Yeongdu looked more pathetic than ever.

The woman, standing with her arms crossed, looked Yeongdu up and down. Her gaze had the power to make you feel awfully small. After a brief exchange of words, the corner of her mouth tilted up. Sajun couldn't make out what she was saying, but she was probably saying something about how pathetic Yeongdu looked. Sajun felt ashamed, as though he himself was the object of her scrutiny. Yeongdu, who had been strangely agitated since back in the dormitory, reacted violently to her words; he shoved her, his face contorted. His push, though, was as weak as that of dry straw.

The woman had been pushed back slightly but showed no reaction other than to brush off the shoulders his hands had touched. She seemed offended, as though something dirty had touched her. The suit jacket that had been draped over her shoulders fell to the ground. She frowned, but she didn't even pick it up, like it didn't matter at all.

That was when things began to get really weird. The woman

mumbled something incomprehensible, and Yeongdu, whose clenched hands had been trembling for some time now, shouted in a loud voice. He was loud enough for Sajun to make out every word.

"Give me the book! I need the book to bring about the Sabbath!"

Losing control of himself, Yeongdu lunged at the woman and began strangling her.

Sajun covered his mouth with his hands. Countless thoughts flashed through his mind in an instant. *What should I do? Should I stop him? But what if I get mixed up in some kind of trouble?* Even at a glance it was obvious that the woman had a lot of money and power. She might sue both Yeongdu and Sajun. Sajun's eyes darted from one spot to another as he anxiously stared at the phone screen. Damn it, he couldn't get caught up in crime for just "fifty-four or more."

As he hesitated, the woman got pushed all the way to the hood of her car. Now half on her back, she struggled with Yeongdu's wrists as he strangled her. The guy was out of his mind. He could kill her for real. Sajun decided that he had to stop him. Just as he was about to push aside the vines and show himself through the window, Yeongdu screamed.

The woman had pulled out a syringe from the inside of her jacket and waved it in the air. The needle was stuck deep in Yeongdu's thin arm. She pushed the plunger all the way down with her thumb. Sajun froze with one leg out the window. Yeongdu's hands fell from her neck.

Yeongdu backed away, cursing and swearing. The woman, leaning against the car, grasped her neck and coughed violently. At the same time, Sajun heaved a deep sigh. He felt dizzy at the thought that he had almost gotten involved in a murder case. Trying to keep himself from flinching, he pulled his leg back inside the building and quietly chanted his spell. Still feeling nervous, however, he began to bite his nails. As he did, a question naturally arose.

What was in that syringe?

Staggering severely, Yeongdu pulled out the syringe that was dangling from his arm and threw it on the ground. His faltering body, unable to avoid any obstacles on the ground, tripped and fell backwards. The woman, whose coughing had ceased, straightened up with a fierce look on her face. She slowly approached Yeongdu. Sitting crumpled on the ground, Yeongdu let out a horrific shriek and backed away.

Sajun began to wonder again if he should stop them. They both seemed to have lost their minds. He had to stop them before he got caught up in something terrible. He wasn't going to ruin his life for some petty amount of money. Having made up his mind, Sajun pushed the vines aside and stepped forward, phone in hand.

"Stop it, both of you! Are you crazy?" he shouted.

As he climbed out through the window, the woman's and Yeongdu's eyes fell on him like daggers. A chill ran down his spine. In that moment, Yeongdu's eyes took on a strange gleam. Leaping to his feet, he shoved the woman aside and came running toward Sajun.

Yeongdu was staggering so severely that he looked as though he would fall any minute. He laughed, both his eyes and mouth wide open. In a hoarse voice he asked, "You—you got it all on video, right?"

Sajun stepped back without even realizing it. He could not grasp what was going on. Clutching his cell phone, which still worked properly, as if it was his lifeline, he stared straight ahead. The camera lens was facing forward. The moment Yeongdu's hand stretched out and touched the tip of his own nose, Sajun heard something that sounded like a watermelon being smashed.

Yeongdu went limp and fell flat on his face. The blood from his head spread out on the dusty ground.

What the woman had swung in the air was a candy cane—sweet candy with alternating red and white stripes. Sajun wondered where the candy cane had come from. It was as big as a real cane, and some of the white parts showed dark red rust. It had probably been a part of a ride. It couldn't be real candy made of sugar. Otherwise Yeongdu's head wouldn't be twisted to the side like that.

The woman looked down at Yeongdu with cold eyes. Someone looking at a rock on the ground would have had more warmth in their eyes. A dark red liquid streaked down the curve of the candy cane. The woman looked unperturbed. Without a change in her expression, she picked up the cane again, as easily as if she was picking up a golf club. Then she took a full swing at Yeongdu's lifeless head, then another, and then another.

Each time the colorful cane swung before his eyes, blood splattered everywhere. Sajun stared at the scene, forgetting how to breathe. It was as unreal as a long-forgotten nightmare. *Clang!* The sound of a solid steel bar hitting the ground pierced his ears.

The woman shook her wrists, looking satisfied as though

she had just finished a bothersome task. Yeongdu, lying on the ground, was no longer moving. Sajun couldn't even be sure if the body lying there was Yeongdu, or a dummy pretending to be a human.

Sajun, who had been staring at the body in a daze, slowly raised his head. The woman, her face devoid of expression, looked him in the eye. As she came up to him, pushing back her blood-splattered hair, all of Sajun's strength left him. His phone slipped to the ground.

The woman's gaze fell on the phone. Sajun shut his eyes tight. Time passed, though he couldn't tell how long—one minute, five minutes, maybe over an hour.

"I like your video," the woman said. Her voice was so calm that he couldn't believe she had just killed someone; there was even a hint of a smile in her words. Sajun opened his eyes slowly. The woman was standing right in front of him, watching the video. He held his breath. When the video came to an end, the woman, still holding the phone in her hand, said, "I'll buy it from you."

She handed him a card. Printed neatly on the crisp white piece of paper were the words, "Gwangnan Cleaning," below which read "Yu Hyeongyeong, CEO." Sajun blinked, and the woman said, smiling, "You've heard of the company, right?"

Sajun nodded slowly. He had heard of it. It was a company that sold cleaning supplies and provided cleaning services. It was one of the country's major cleaning companies. Thinking back, Sajun remembered seeing her on television from time to time. She looked him in the eyes as he sat on the ground. Looking at her bloody face, Sajun felt faint.

His mind stopped functioning. He had no idea what to make of what had just happened and what was about to happen. The woman proposed a simple solution.

"No need to make it complicated. I'll make sure you get compensated fairly."

Compensated. Hearing the word, he began to think again, as though his dead mind had come back to life. What she meant by compensation had to be money, and compensation by someone so rich and famous was bound to be incomparable with Yeong-du's 540,000 won.

What's in my account plus fifty-four or more, and more and more and more ... Sajun recalled his familiar spell. The number of zeroes in his head inflated and deflated like a broken calculator. Maybe the compensation would be so big that the numbers in his magic spell would look like nothing in comparison.

He couldn't hide the feeling of excitement that flitted through his heart. He guessed that such feelings—in the face of a psychopath who didn't even care to wipe the blood off her face—violated the norms or ethics of society, but fuck, who cared? He had just happened to end up where he was. He was a poor little shrimp who had got dragged into this fight between whales. So accepting the proffered compensation would be the reasonable thing to do. It seemed that positive hormones were being released from a corner of his brain. What he was doing, though, was more like myopic rationalization than positive thinking.

His hands were no longer trembling. His dazed pupils regained their focus. Sajun raised his head and looked the woman in the face. She grinned like someone from a commercial. Sajun nodded his head.

The New Seoul Park Jelly Massacre

Sajun loaded Yeongdu's dead body into Director Yu's trunk. Feeling uncomfortable, he gently closed Yeongdu's eyes, which had been wide open.

Yu took out a bottle of bleach from the trunk and poured some onto the bloodstained ground. As the blood and bleach mingled, the dark red blood turned an odd color. Sajun flinched when he saw her picking up the candy cane. Their eyes met, but she didn't even bat an eye.

After cleaning up the crime scene, Yu got into the driver's seat. Sajun sat in the passenger seat. The imported luxury car glided smoothly through the narrow mountain path. Sajun glanced at Yu as she drove. There was an unmistakable smile on her lips.

Had it felt that terrific to kill Yeongdu? Sajun realized that he knew nothing about their relationship, but he didn't dare ask. He didn't even want to know. Receiving cash was more important to him than receiving information that he probably couldn't process. The two drove on without a word as the car moved along the mountain path. The sound of people screaming on the rides came from a distance like an echo. The car came to a stop in front of a thickly wooded area. They couldn't go any further by car.

"It's private ground so there shouldn't be anyone around," Yu said.

Sajun climbed up the mountain for a while with the dead body on his back before beginning to dig a hole in the ground. He was dripping with sweat. The only thing he could hear was the sound of leaves rustling. Every now and then, the wind brought the echoing sound of people screaming in the theme park. As Sajun continued to dig a hole, Yu stood at a distance, fiddling with a tablet PC. She acted as if she had nothing to do with the dead body. She burst into a fit of laughter after staring at the screen for a while. The sound gave him the chills. He quietly went on with his task. He resented her for not even lifting a finger to help, but he didn't want to rub her the wrong way by saying something he shouldn't. He wasn't an idiot like Yeongdu.

Only after digging a hole deep enough to satisfy Yu did he throw Yeongdu's dead body into it. Seeing how his head was bent at a strange angle, Sajun shivered. Yeongdu's eyes, which he had closed for him, were wide open again. Trying to shake off an awful feeling, Sajun scattered a handful of dirt over Yeongdu's face.

Yu made her way slowly over to the hole and threw in the candy cane, which she had wiped clean with bleach. The colorful steel bar fell onto Yeongdu's chest with a thud. Yeongdu's body, shaking from the impact, looked alive to Sajun, as though it had gone into a spasm. Having finished her business, Yu pointed to the hole with her chin, and Sajun picked up the shovel again. Every muscle in his body ached. The exhaustion and pain were proof that he wasn't dreaming. Yeongdu's death, the psychopath behind him, the compensation to come—all of it was real.

In haste, he began to fill the pit with dirt. It was much easier than digging the hole. The thought of Yeongdu's wide-open eyes gave him a headache. Sajun began to hum the numbers and tune that were familiar to him.

"I have 180 coming in for my monthly pay, plus overtime pay for the extra parade, minus ten for phone and internet and twenty for food; let's say thirty for living expenses; then I should have about x left. Add that to the money in my account, and I should have x; plus what I made today, plus fifty-four or more, and more and more and more …"

The numbers accumulated as he rattled off various expenses and petty incomes. His face was full of excitement. Yeongdu's wide-open eyes no longer had a place in his mind.

The luxury car made its way back down the path. Feeling anxious, Sajun fidgeted with his fingertips. As the music from the theme park grew closer, he began to think of serious words that were relevant in the real world: crime, murder, and accomplice. At the same time, the rumor about Yeongdu being the personnel manager's nephew flashed through his mind. He opened his mouth cautiously.

"What if someone makes a report? I'll be the first one under suspicion …" he said.

The car screeched to a sudden halt. His body was propelled forward before regaining balance with difficulty. Yu gazed at him, looking as immaculate as she had when she had first shown up. No one would see her as anything but a capable CEO, someone far from committing murder. Like a boss instructing a new recruit on the most basic task, she said clearly in a kind voice, "There's no murder without a body. We were lucky in that respect—the person we buried has no family or relatives. There's nothing for you to worry about."

Taken aback, Sajun said, "But I heard that he was the personnel manager's nephew. That's why he didn't get fired even when he got into trouble …."

Yu snorted, a knowing look on her face. Then she pulled out the tablet PC from her briefcase and handed it to him.

"The rumor is false. What kind of connection do you need anyway, for a part-time job as a mascot?"

Sajun looked at the screen. It showed all kinds of personal data and information on Yeongdu. Just as Yu had said, he had no family to speak of. An indescribable emptiness washed over Sajun. All the feelings he had harbored toward Yeongdu—all the malice and feelings of inferiority—had been for nothing. Only then did he finally grasp the reality of what he had done; he had buried a human being in the ground. *Oh, what have I done?* He wondered, staring at his dirt-covered hands. A bitter laugh slipped from his lips.

"Ha ha …"

The car began to move again along the rugged path. Yu mumbled something, looking enraptured. She sounded as careful as someone confessing her love, but her voice was full of confidence. "I knew it—he is on my side."

Sajun looked out the window. The sky was turning red. Sajun and Director Yu returned to the theme park, each with a different smile on their face.

*

Sajun took the envelope from Director Yu with a trembling hand. The envelope was so thick that he could barely hold it in one hand. The moment he felt the weight of the envelope in his palm, a curious sense of peace washed over him. Yu added these enticing words, though Sajun couldn't tell if she was saying them out of courtesy or if she meant them seriously: "Call me if you need more."

Sajun seemed to see bloodstains overlapping her graciously smiling face. He clutched the envelope of money to his chest. The red afterimage he had just seen wasn't real; it was an illusion. So were the events that had happened earlier. They were all illusions. But the heavy, smooth feel of the envelope at his fingertips was real. He cracked open the envelope and peeked inside. His heart began to beat fast again when he saw the yellow of the fifty-thousand won bills. Sajun made a deep bow to Yu, then jumped out of the car and began to run as fast as he could.

"How much money do I have in my account? Plus my monthly pay … and the money in this envelope …"

He smelled something sweet. The whole time he ran, he repeated his spell over and over. The spell, chanted in rhythm to the sound of his heavy breathing and the beat of his rushing footsteps, was like a gentle song.

Back in his dorm room, Sajun hid the money in a hurry. Spotting Yeongdu's box, he emptied it out and put the money in it. He shoved all the creepy sheets of paper in the trash. By the time he had changed out of his soiled clothes and put things roughly in order, it was nearing eight o'clock in the evening. He remembered that there would be a night parade today since it was the weekend.

*

Once again, Sajun began to run. The parade started at eight on the dot. He had to be ready to go, lined up for the parade, by ten minutes to eight. It was 7:50 now. He hastily pushed open the door to the changing room and stuffed himself into the Dream Teddy suit.

He was about to step outside with Dream Teddy's head under his arm but had a hard time moving his feet for some reason. He looked down at his feet. He couldn't see anything—the lights seemed to have gone out. He bent down and lifted one foot and saw a mysterious lump stretching out, like cheese on a pizza right out of the oven.

He had no time to lose. The parade was about to start. He anxiously shook his foot. Finally managing to free himself from the slime, he ran straight outside. He saw the main square where the parade would start and where he danced and handed out balloons every day.

He put on Dream Teddy's head, which he had been carrying under his arm. He succeeded in aligning his eyes with the slits which showed through the wide-open mouth of Dream Teddy. He turned his head slowly. There was no line for the parade. He looked up at the clock tower. It was three minutes after eight. Three minutes had passed from the appointed hour. There was no parade music playing. Only then did he realize that it was exceptionally quiet around him. Not only was there no music, but there was no laughter or shouting, or screaming either. Sajun stood still.

He pulled off Dream Teddy's head. As he did, the air rushed into his nose along with a sweet smell. He stared at the scene in front of him. "*Sticky, pink hell.*" The words the manager had uttered with an exaggerated look on his face flashed through his mind. Sajun said the words out loud: "Sticky, pink hell."

His voice was cracked. So he was still able to hear. It was so quiet around him that it frightened him. As he said the words, "sticky, pink hell," a glob of pink slime dangling from a streetlamp fell with a plop—right onto Dream Teddy's bulging belly.

It was exactly as the words described. The theme park was submerged in a massive sea of jelly. Globs of mysterious pink jelly were covering up this place of dream and fantasy. Everything was full of jelly—from the rollercoaster that had stopped at its starting point to the pirate ship that wasn't swinging up and down—as if someone had scooped it up and poured it onto the rides. Sajun stared at the clothes, bags, all sorts of shoes, and other discarded things that were scattered everywhere. Nothing remained but jelly and these items; there was not a sign of a person anywhere. In silence, he faced the scene before him. There was nothing more he could do.

The Mascot Cat

I've lived for many years. The human who picked me up off the street and took me home died, and her daughter went off somewhere. The house where we used to live remained for a long time even after it fell into ruin. But in the end, it was torn down by an enormous machine, leaving me there all alone.

Cement was poured onto the debris of the house. Many humans and machines came and went as they put up a new building. I saw with my own eyes how everything—the street where the old human and I used to take walks, the hill that she had loved, and the hideout I used to sneak out to so I could see my friends from the streets—disappeared in an instant. I wasn't all that sad since I knew that I would live for a long time yet and that the new buildings, too, would crumble away someday. Humans are always tearing down old things and raising up new things. They'll probably tear down this world someday.

Changes came and went, and the sadness in my heart faded away. I forgot how to form an attachment to things. To live for a very long time, I had to get used to forgetting things.

As I lived longer and longer, old memories were replaced with new ones, and with each passing day there were more and more things I couldn't recall even though I wanted to. Clues that would bring them back to me didn't last forever either. I couldn't help but feel empty inside as I thought about all the moments of my life fading away like that. What was I, after all, if all the memories that made me up were gone?

I wonder if it's different for humans. Can they remember fleeting moments? Storing shards of memories may be an easy task for them since they're always coming up with useful new machines. But if it is possible for them, how do they live with so many wounds and scars in their hearts?

Every once in a while, I think about the old woman's daughter who left her mother behind. The daughter often annoyed me when she was young. She would give me a bath when I didn't want one; she would shake a foxtail in my face; she would tickle my face and belly. Memories are strange things. When you reminisce on things over and over again, you're left in the end with moments you want to return to.

I wonder where the girl is now, what she's doing. Does she remember the tuxedo cat who lived with her when she was young? Or did she forget all about the cat and everything else the moment she left home? I hope it's the latter. It's a very lonely thing to live in the past. I hope she isn't lonely.

I've lived for many years. And for those many years, I've stayed where I used to live with the old woman and her daughter. That red brick house no longer exists. In its place is a tacky and flashy theme park called New Seoul Park. That's where I live.

The New Seoul Park Jelly Massacre

Why haven't I left this place? I'm not sure. What is it that I'm waiting for? Everything seems so remote—I remember less and less as time goes by.

In the early days of the park, I hid in places like the mountain behind the park or in a storage building. No good would come from letting humans see me. I'd rather be alone than be with someone who leaves as easily as they came. But as people began to come and go, I kept exposing myself without meaning to, and they didn't leave me alone.

They called me Dream Kitty. I didn't like the name at all. Dream Kitty—oh, please. The furry creature that's always busy shaking its rump in this park is called Dream Teddy. I was quite insulted to be categorized with a lowly creature like that. When those who called me Dream Kitty offered me snacks, I didn't even touch them.

My days in New Seoul Park were peaceful. The place was always full of people, loud music, and sweet smells. I didn't have to worry about food because everyone who came to the park was dying to feed me. I picked and chose from what they offered me. My favorite was tuna and salmon. Thanks to all the food, I became so much fatter than I used to be when I lived with the old human.

In the summer, I'd go inside a cool building and take a nap, and in the winter, I'd warm myself inside a heated building. Every building I went into had a soft cushion and food ready for me.

That day was a little strange. I've lived for many years, but never has there been a day so strange. I didn't have a very hard time coming to terms with the old human dying and the red brick house being torn down in an instant, but that day was something I couldn't understand for the life of me.

It was an unusually hot day, but I didn't feel like going inside a building. So I just sat still, watching people pass by. Then I noticed something. The furry creature that always danced with a stupid look on its face took off its head and revealed what was inside. Narrowing my eyes, I stared at the curious scene. Standing in the middle of the square, the human was uttering curses, sweating profusely. I couldn't believe my eyes and ears. It was a sort of taboo to expose what was inside the furry suit. An invisible rupture was taking place. Something was going wrong.

And then there was the smell. New Seoul Park was always full of sweet smells, but the smell that day was of a different kind. I'm not sure how to describe it. Usually the smell was light and lukewarm; that day, it was heavy and stale. I couldn't even take a nap, which was a very serious problem. I moved to a different spot several times, but the awful feeling of suffocation wouldn't leave me.

In the end, I made my way over to a bench in the shadow of a tree and settled down under it. Four short legs came into my view. Two human children were talking to each other. Quietly, I listened to their voices. One of them was a crybaby, and the other sounded too mature for a little child.

Both of them seemed to have lost their parents. A lot of children got lost in the park. If there was no one around to help, I usually led these children to the mushroom-shaped house called the Lost Children Center. It was quite a bother, but I got myself up to do the same once again. As I did, I saw the hem of a fluttering blue dress approaching from a distance. The

The New Seoul Park Jelly Massacre

grown-up woman who came rushing over took the crybaby into her arms and broke into tears.

Should I help or not? I wondered, poking my head out to look at the mature child. She was clenching her little hands, again with an unchildlike expression on her face. She looked like the old woman's daughter on the day she had left home.

I slipped out from under the bench. I wished that the child would get angry. At least that would mean that she was showing her true feelings. If you keep your feelings pent up inside, the weight of them makes you feel lonely.

I followed the crybaby, walking hand in hand with the woman, and the other child who was walking by herself, a little apart from them. Something on the crybaby's head sparkled in the light. I had seen something like it before, an ornament that the old woman had cherished and the only thing her daughter took with her when she left home. A little sigh escaped my mouth, but I didn't feel much of anything. Just because you remember something doesn't mean that you feel the warmth and affection you experienced at that moment. Feelings are lighter than memories and fly away much faster. The memories of those days were still there, but they, too, would vanish with time.

The wavy-haired woman in a blue dress had sunken red eyes. So did the child with the pin in her hair. I looked from one to the other. I wanted to recall the face of the old human's daughter, but those days were so long ago that I couldn't remember. The woman and the children went into a café. I sat on the rail of the café terrace, watching them.

The crybaby was no longer crying. The mature child was just a child now. I let out a long yawn, puzzled at myself for worrying about someone else and not just resting in the heat. I wondered why I was taking the trouble to do so, when this moment, too, would soon be forgotten. Then a long shadow was cast over me. I raised my head and saw a man in a familiar uniform. He was the man who had been giving out jelly here and there in the park. There was nothing remarkable about him, but every time our eyes met, I felt strangely uneasy. The man patted me on the back. I didn't like it; and at the same time, I instinctively knew that he wasn't human. With a faint smile on his face he whispered, "You've been living here for a long time."

His voice sounded as though it had come crawling out from the deepest part of the world. All the hair on my body stood on end. I extended my claws and hissed at the man. Still smiling, the man, who had a hat pulled down low over his face, said in a quiet voice: "You'll see, something fun is about to happen."

Then he disappeared. When I looked over at the café again, the mature child was dropping a jelly in the crybaby's drink. Sparkling like a jewel, the jelly began to dissolve. I had a feeling that something terrible was going to happen. The hunch of a long-lived animal is usually right.

Humans melted away. Like all the things they tore down, they melted away into nothing. Only lumps of pink jelly, the color of the soles of my paws, remained in New Seoul Park. With each step I took came a new pawprint. All alone, I roamed the park, without a single person in sight, watching my pawprints appear

The New Seoul Park Jelly Massacre

and disappear. I was alone again. I have lived for a very long time and will live for a very long time yet.

Time passed and dust piled up on top of all the jelly. I walked around in the middle of the theme park, where there was no more music, or furry creatures dancing, or people giving me food. I wasn't sure if I should stay, or where I should go if I didn't.

That was when I heard a voice behind me.

Our First Day Together

<u>D-DAY</u>

Da-ae felt as if she was dreaming. She was surrounded by upbeat music, colorful rides, Dream Teddy handing out balloons to kids, Dream Teddy's brightly smiling friends, well-manicured flowerbeds, and a sweet, pleasant smell. And above all, Jaeyun was standing by her side. Everything was perfect. She was even happy that the day was so hot, with a record high temperature. She preferred extreme over average.

The sky was clear with a blazing sun, and the trees fresh and green. Da-ae hoped that the way she was feeling now and the memories of this moment wouldn't fade away until the day she died. She hoped that Jaeyun felt the same way. She turned her head to look at him. He had his eyes trained on something else. She tightened her grip on his hand. He turned around and looked at her. Da-ae said in an exaggerated voice, "I've never been to a theme park before! This is so much fun!"

Jaeyun smiled. Although his lips were turned up in a smile, his eyes looked tense, and beads of sweat trickled down his flushed face. Da-ae turned away, trying to ignore the shadow on his face. She didn't let go of his hand. She had no intention of letting go, not today. Her hand grew damp.

Each time his hand was about to slip out of hers, she clutched it tight. The small sighs that escaped his lips evaporated before ever reaching her ears. Or perhaps they did reach her ears—they just failed to have any effect on her.

As Da-ae looked around, something interesting caught her eye. A man in a uniform was standing in front of a small, tented stall handing out packets of jelly. Da-ae pulled Jaeyun by the hand.

"Let's go look over there," she said.

"Okay," Jaeyun said, nodding along absentmindedly.

The man, noticing the two coming toward him, picked up what was on the stall counter and shouted, "We have brand-new jelly here! Come try it out! You can't find this flavor anywhere else in the world!"

Neither Da-ae nor Jaeyun had heard of the brand before. The palm-sized packets contained mouthwatering jelly, which showed through the clear middle part of the packets. The jelly probably smelled like fresh fruit and had an artificial sweet flavor, and the white powder covering the jelly was probably sour. The man handed them a packet, and Da-ae took it without hesitation. Seeming pleased, the man looked from Jaeyun to Da-ae.

"What a beautiful couple you are! This jelly will keep you from ever breaking up. It's magic jelly. You'll be inseparable for the rest of your life, I promise," he said, making a great fuss.

"Really? Jaeyun, did you hear what he said? He's hilarious!" Da-ae said, laughing excessively. Jaeyun just nodded, not showing much of a reaction. Da-ae took the packet of jelly from the man and put it in her bag.

The New Seoul Park Jelly Massacre

"Thank you. I hope you have a good day," she said to the man.

Jaeyun and Da-ae passed the stall and walked on. They got on what was supposed to be the scariest ride in New Seoul Park, and then went through the haunted house. When they got tired, they stopped for churros and ice cream at the café.

Something was wrong with Jaeyun. Normally, he would be quite chatty, saying let's do this, let's not do that; but today, he was just going along with everything Da-ae said. He was like a deflated balloon.

They finally got up from their seats as the last bit of ice cream melted away. After walking for a while, they found themselves in front of the carousel. They had fallen into silence. To break the uncomfortable awkwardness, Da-ae rummaged through her bag. Her hand came across the packet of jelly she had gotten earlier. Turning it over, she said, "Jaeyun, do you want some jelly? What brand is this anyway? I've never heard of it. I don't think it's famous."

"Da-ae," said Jaeyun in a heavy voice.

"Yeah?" Da-ae said with a sinking feeling in her heart.

"Let's break up."

Darkness fell over Da-ae's eyes. The two stood facing each other without a word. As the park turned orange in the glow of the setting sun, colorful lights came on. The carousel went round and round as the music played.

D-1000 (or more)

It was my grandfather who named me Da-ae. "Da" stands for "a lot," and "ae" for "love." He wanted me to be someone who was full of love for others. I don't remember much about him. He passed away when I was very young. The only thing I remember is that his voice sounded scary when he called out to me, waving his arm, thin as a branch of an old tree. I never answered him when he called, not even once.

But anyway, I liked my name. Love is a good thing, and the more you have of a good thing, the better. But a name was just a name—my life wasn't any different from anyone else's. I wasn't especially full of love. I was as selfish as anyone and often looked the other way, pretending not to have noticed someone in need. I had dated several guys since high school, but there had been no one special.

During my adolescence, I had worried quite a bit because I felt that I lacked emotion. It wasn't that I had a problem feeling things such as alienation and inferiority, or sadness and distress, or pleasure and sorrow. I just wasn't passionate about relationships. My relationships with my friends and my parents weren't bad, but that was it. I vaguely knew that one day, I would grow distant from everyone.

I often wondered, though. Where did all that love in my name go? Could I someday be that person full of love, as my grandfather had hoped?

D-500

It was in Noryangjin, the "exam town," that I met Jaeyun. After graduating from a private university, I had been preparing for the teacher certification exam, and Jaeyun had been studying for the level-nine civil servant exam. We lived on different floors of the same gosiwon, an accommodation building for students preparing for exams. The building had been renovated from an old multiplex house. The floors were divided between guys and girls, except for the kitchen and the laundry room, which everyone used together.

Living in the same building with someone, you were bound to run into them from time to time. On top of that, since people who lived in a gosiwon all attended similar classes for similar purposes, you often ran into someone you had seen around your neighborhood at educational institutes. That had been the case for Jaeyun and me. We had seen each other around but hadn't had a chance to say hello. One day, I was having a late meal in the kitchen, when Jaeyun asked, "Can I sit with you?"

I thought he had a nice voice. I felt as if a gentle wave was washing over my ears. That night, I saw my grandfather in my dream for some reason. I had long forgotten what he looked like, but I could tell from the silhouette; and I just had a feeling that it was him. He reached out a strong, solid arm, no longer thin as a branch, and called out my name: "Da-ae."

Although it was a dream, I answered him, for the first time. I wasn't afraid. When I opened my eyes, only goosebumps remained, and a strange sense of awareness.

Jaeyun and I became fast friends after that one conversation. He was much more outgoing than I was and had a knack for putting people at ease. We often shared a table and food. After a few more conversations, we found out that we attended different academies in the same building.

The next day, during independent study hour, Jaeyun texted me saying that he had something for me. My heart trembled more violently than it did when I had gotten my mock test scores back. At the fire escape where we met, he held out a vitamin drink—the kind I always had. I drank it habitually to fight off sleep, but that day it had seemed terribly special. It wasn't the first time someone had given me a little gift, but it had been different somehow. I hadn't ever felt that way before.

D-440

My life has been a smooth ride for the most part because I went along with the efforts and demands of my parents, who wanted me to live a stable and secure life. Preparing to be a teacher was a part of those efforts. Studying for the exam was difficult, but I hadn't had any great failures in my life, so I was confident that I could reach my goal. A life with no failures. I'm not saying that I was born a genius or that I came from a well-off family. What I'm saying is that I had never genuinely wanted for anything.

My mom talked about my grandfather from time to time. She didn't have anything nice to say about him. It was mostly idle complaining about how he lost a fortune through gambling when he was young, and how otherwise, we would be living in a ritzy apartment in Gangnam by now. What stood out to me, though, was something else. I committed to my memory the principles of gambling: if you bet little you lose little; if you bet big you lose big. Rarely does anyone bet little and win big.

I thought I was betting very timidly on the issues of life. I always expected little from life because I didn't have the courage to bet anything big. I only hoped for inconsequential things that wouldn't affect me at all if I lost them. That was the kind of life my mom wanted for me and the kind of life I wanted for myself. But after I met Jaeyun, the tranquil surface of my life began to shake.

Jaeyun was the only thing that brought a sparkle into my life as I lived in the gosiwon. We met at the fire escape every lunch break. After having lunch together, he would head to the sixth floor for his class, and I would head to the seventh for mine. After our classes, we returned to the gosiwon together, sometimes taking a longer way around.

One day, we came out of the building and felt the freshness of the cold air. Without either of us saying anything about it, we passed the alley we should have taken and took a walk around the neighborhood. We chatted about this and that. Still not wanting to say goodbye, we went into a convenience store. We bought two cans of beer and a bag of snacks and went back the way we had come.

From the roof of the gosiwon, which stood on a hill, you could get a night view of the town. There were clusters of light, and the sound of drunk people shouting mingled with the sound of stray cats meowing. We sat side by side, both of us in sweat suits, drinking beer. The silence that followed wasn't awkward. Gazing at Jaeyun as he drew nearer, I thought about the name my grandfather had given me and about the money he must have staked when gambling. I felt as if I had staked something so big that I couldn't handle it. We kissed, with a night view—though it wasn't very beautiful—spread out before us.

D-400

The old bed in the gosiwon was so small that the two of us could barely sit together on it. Our eyes were on a little palm-sized television with a bulky back, so outdated that I had no idea how old it was. A theme park commercial for special price tickets was playing on the screen with a lot of static. A character—a bear or a mouse, I couldn't tell—set off a firecracker, and colorful sparks exploded in the night sky, spelling out the words, NEW SEOUL PARK OPEN AT A SPECIAL PRICE.

"How pretty. I haven't been to a theme park since I was a kid," I mumbled absently.

Jaeyun looked into my eyes and said, "We should go, then."

"Really? When?"

"When we've both passed our exams."

I wanted to touch the slightly upturned corner of his mouth. The commercial soon came to an end, but firecrackers kept going off in my mind.

The firecrackers became bigger and more spectacular when I came home after class and lay down in my bed, having read test materials that seemed more and more meaningless to me as time went on. The rides that made your heart palpitate, the childish but cute masks, the sweet candies and jelly, the upbeat music and the parades. I studied night and day, picturing the day when I would go enjoy them.

The New Seoul Park Jelly Massacre

D-370

I wanted to be able to enjoy more things together with Jaeyun. The theme park commercial had quickly intensified that desire. To achieve my goal, I had to escape this horrid town, with Jaeyun by my side, of course. I devoted myself to my studies, which I had neglected for a while because of the doubts I'd been having. I believed that Jaeyun felt the same way.

I was pacing around the corridor, drinking instant coffee to fight off drowsiness. I heard the instructor next door grilling a student: "What's wrong with your grades? Are you too busy dating or something?"

The student said nothing, head bowed. I smiled without meaning to. Then I looked at my name at the top of the mock test results on the bulletin board. Looking at my name printed proudly at the top, I wondered if someone like me could really be a teacher, but then again, probably not everyone chose their profession with a great sense of responsibility. I told myself that I could do it.

That afternoon, my instructor at the institute summoned me to the office. He handed me an application form for a special weekend night class, saying, "You weren't making any progress for a while, but your grades have gone up dramatically. You can pass the exam this time."

That'll leave me with even less time to see Jaeyun was the first thought that came to my mind.

I hesitated for a bit, but in the end, I signed the form. Passing the exam and getting out of this awful place was something I wanted as well. To get two marshmallows later, I had to forgo the one marshmallow in front of me.

I came out of the office and looked down at the city through the corridor window. I spotted someone familiar, though I could only see his back. The person walking into a convenience store with a girl I didn't know was, without a doubt, Jaeyun. They came out together after a little while. The girl was holding a vitamin drink in her hand.

That November, I passed the first part of the teacher certification exam. So why wasn't I happy?

D-270

Jaeyun had failed the supplementary exam held in October. He congratulated me nonetheless, smiling and saying, "I'll study harder and pass the exam soon."

I believed him. There's nothing wrong with believing someone, is there?

While Jaeyun was in the restroom I picked up his cell phone. I knew his password. I had seen a suspicious look cross his face when he had checked his phone after hearing it buzz. As soon as I entered the password, the screen showed a text message from a girl I didn't know.

The message read: "Who are you drinking with? Do you want me to come?"

Still smiling, I deleted the message.

D-200

I passed the interview without a problem. I got my final letter of acceptance, but I couldn't really celebrate when someone close to me had failed the first part of his exam. Jaeyun, after failing the level-nine exam two years in a row, seemed overcome by a sense of defeat. He congratulated me in a feeble voice. I didn't feel happy. I had pictured this moment so many times, but this wasn't how I had imagined I would feel when I finally made it— not at all. I chewed the steak, which felt dry, unable to enjoy the taste.

We parted early. Jaeyun said he had to go back to the institute and study. I nodded my head.

D-150

We met less and less often after I got assigned to a school as a teacher. I was busy with various trainings and tasks. I got even busier after being assigned as a homeroom teacher. The kids, who were still in the process of growth and refinement, were too raw for me to handle. I didn't feel a sense of responsibility, either. When the other teachers who had gotten their assignments at the same time I had talked about what adorable troublemakers their students were, I didn't know what to say. I had nothing to say because I didn't feel anything toward my students. I never showed much of a reaction when they got into trouble or brought me little gifts. They soon lost any interest they had in me. Kids that age are quite perceptive, precisely because they are so raw.

Although I spent a lot of time at school, I didn't have the time to think about my students. I felt anxious whenever I thought of Jaeyun. Was this how people felt when they bet a lot of money and didn't have a good hand? They could just stop playing, of course, but it wouldn't be gambling if they could just walk out when they wanted, would it? Then one day, Jaeyun called me early in the morning, drunk.

"Da-ae, you're not going to leave me, are you?" Jaeyun asked, crying.

After hanging up, I laughed out loud for the first time in a while. I found him unbearably adorable for worrying about nothing. The morning news was playing on the LED television—a latest model that defied comparison with the television at the gosiwon.

STUDENT PREPARING FOR A CIVIL SERVANT EXAM COMMITS SUICIDE ON ROOFTOP, the caption read.

The location had been deliberately blurred, but anyone who had lived in the neighborhood could easily tell where it was. It was the institute Jaeyun and I had attended. The sad headline disappeared in less than three minutes and was replaced by another. I stared at the bluish screen until the news came to an end. I hoped that Jaeyun would become even more vulnerable.

D-120

We were happy again. I somehow managed to make the time to go to Noryangjin at least twice a week. Jaeyun, tired from years of preparing for his exam, became more and more exhausted and irritable. He would push me away, then lean on me completely like a child if we grew even slightly distant. I took him out for nice meals and bought him decent clothes. He was reluctant at first, but as time passed, he accepted everything without hesitation. And he showered me with sweet words, like a machine that speaks when you insert a coin.

"I love you so much," he would say, along with other things that may sound like clichés but mean everything to some people.

D-110

A coffee break with the other teachers always included time spent blabbing about the principal and the vice-principal. No matter where you work, there was bound to be an old geezer or two who would try to dump their work on a young and powerless new recruit. The conversations always took pretty much the same turn. We would talk about our bosses, then start talking about our love lives. As a result we knew all about who any one of us was dating, even though we weren't that close. The music teacher sitting across from me, in particular, was especially interested in other people's business.

"You have so much love in you, Da-ae. Is it because of your name?"

"I heard that the character 'ae' makes you attract all kinds of crazies."

"Forget about that boyfriend of yours. He's still just a student preparing for an exam. Lots of great guys have their eyes on you, so why are you still with him?"

The others chimed in, taking their cue from the music teacher. I just smiled a little without saying anything. Since we belonged to the same education office in the same district, we would be seeing each other around for a long time to come as we went from one school to another; saying the wrong thing could make things difficult later on. Whenever I was put in these situations, though, I felt overwhelmed by a feeling of doubt that I couldn't explain. I felt as though I was suffocating underwater as I wondered how long I would have to put up with everything, my feelings bottled up inside, trying to be agreeable all the time with an awkward smile on my face. Hiding behind an innocent smile, I cursed and swore at them in my mind. People who didn't understand my love, people who didn't know anything, were saying mindless things about Jaeyun and me.

I'm not like you people. We're different.

My name became nothing but food for gossip on their lips. Whenever I felt that something I cherished was being tainted, I just put up with it, smiling and smiling until I was sick of it. They had only one thing right: I did have a lot of love in me.

<u>D-75</u>

Time passed.

<u>D-30</u>

The day came at last. Jaeyun passed his exam. Talking to him on the phone, I happily burst out sobbing. I was even happier than when I had passed my own exam.

"What time should we meet?" I asked.

"Huh?"

"We have to celebrate together, on a day like this. I'll come as soon as I get off work."

"Um, Da-ae, today isn't good for me because my parents are coming up to Seoul."

"I can't see you, not even for a moment?"

"Not today, sorry."

After we hung up, I returned to the teachers' room and stared blankly at my desk. There were piles of various notices and papers I had to take care of. I didn't want to even look at them. I stood up and headed to my homeroom class. I passed several kids who didn't say hello even when our eyes met, and arrived at the last room at the end of the hallway. I heard kids talking inside.

"What do you think of our homeroom teacher? She doesn't know what she's doing, does she? She sucks at teaching."

"I wonder if she even knows our names."

The kids snickered. I went back the way I had come. The vice-principal came to the teachers' room and asked me something, but I didn't answer him, my face set hard. I couldn't say a word. I felt that if I opened my mouth, I would blurt out something I would regret. Ignoring the vice-principal's nagging, I left in a hurry as soon as the bell rang.

I headed to Noryangjin with a cake in my hand. When I opened the old gosiwon door and entered, a strange feeling—a longing for the past or something, I couldn't really tell—came over me. I felt that I was happier back when I was running at full speed with my goal in sight. And back then, Jaeyun and I had felt the same amount of affection for each other. I headed upstairs to

Jaeyun's room. He would come sooner or later if I waited inside. The owner of the gosiwon, sitting in the maintenance office, recognized me and called out, "Hi Da-ae, it's been a while!"

She then went on to talk about herself for a bit, after which her eyes fell on the cake in my hand. Smiling, I said, "It's for Jaeyun—he passed his exam."

"Oh, didn't you two break up?" she asked, her eyes wide open.

My heart sank.

"What do you mean, break up?" I asked.

"Oh, well, I … I thought you broke up, because Jaeyun … Oh, what am I saying."

She stopped talking and rushed away, looking awkward. I went up to Jaeyun's room. He wasn't there. I waited inside for a long time. I texted him but got no reply. I ended up leaving at around ten o'clock. I left the cake sitting in the room and headed to the subway station.

The woman's words kept tugging at my mind. When you have anticipated something, it always turns out to be a far cry from what you expected. That was the case on the day I had found out that I'd passed my exam, then on my first day at work, and this time as well.

I was passing through the alleys I knew by heart—alleys I was sick and tired of—when I heard a familiar voice. I turned my head automatically. It was Jaeyun. He was talking, completely drunk, with some friends I had seen a few times before. I knew it would be better to go up to him and talk to him face to face, but my finger pressed his speed dial number as if it had a mind of its own.

The phone rang. I saw Jaeyun in the distance, pulling out

his phone from his pocket. Then the signal went dead. Frowning, he put the phone back in his pocket. I went on my way, as though I hadn't seen anything. I took the subway and returned to my studio apartment. I waited till past midnight, but he never called.

D-15

Having passed the exam, Jaeyun began to prepare for the interview with a study group. I didn't hear from him much, as he said he was even busier than when he had been studying for the exam. He was the one preparing for the interview, but I was the one who felt strangely anxious. I spent all day checking his Instagram, biting my nails. Whenever I saw him doing something I hadn't known about, a deep sense of defeat washed over me.

An update notification popped up. A new post had been added: a photo with the words, "Let's all pass the interview!" The three other people in the square photo were from Jaeyun's study group. All three of them were girls. I stopped biting my nails. I felt numb and couldn't move. Drops of blood fell from my tattered nails.

D-7

Jaeyun was nice to me all of a sudden. It made me nervous. I was aware that something was very wrong with this relationship. But I didn't have the courage to find out for sure.

D-3

I was looking out the window. It was raining. For the first time in a while, Jaeyun had said he wanted to meet. We went to a café and talked about this and that. We used to meet like this often, but this time, the lulls in our conversations felt extremely awkward. I turned my head to the window, unable to break the silence. Jaeyun thrust his phone at me and said, "How about we go to a theme park this weekend? You said before that you wanted to go."

I felt a tingling in my heart.

"Do you mean that?" I asked.

Jaeyun nodded. His phone screen showed a ticket that said "Couple's Package." My heart began to flutter. The commercial I'd seen long ago at the gosiwon began to replay in my mind. I recalled the atmosphere around us at the time, the warmth in Jaeyun's eyes as we talked, and even the musty smell of mold that had permeated the room.

I felt as though I had gone back in time. I could feel my eyes shining with excitement. New Seoul Park, a place of hopes and dreams—I imagined that there would be nothing but fun and pleasure there, that the place was like an igloo made of sugar, which no misfortune in the world could infiltrate.

I knew that that was impossible. Everything that shines and sparkles in a theme park has simply just been designed with great care. But … there's no harm in believing, is there?

The New Seoul Park Jelly Massacre

D-DAY

"But why?" Da-ae asked.

"You know as well as I do that things aren't the same anymore. We' re both doing well now, so let's just end it here," Jaeyun replied.

An awkward silence fell between the two. Da-ae's lips moved slightly, but she couldn't say anything. She didn't know what to say, or how she should say it. She felt as though a big fish bone was stuck in her throat.

Jaeyun went off, saying he had to go to the restroom. Da-ae stood there alone in a daze. Her face looked calm but her heart was in turmoil. What had happened during the past five hundred days or so flashed before her eyes. The days that had made her heart sting a little now and then were now jabbing at her heart, as if to say that they had full power now.

She couldn't believe what Jaeyun had said. That was why she wasn't even crying. She had ignored all the signs. This must be how one feels when an ominous prophecy begins to come true step by step: powerless to prevent anything, even though you know what is about to take place, and shocked at the crumbling world inside you. No one could easily accept a situation like that. Her feelings of defiance soon turned to rage.

"You know as well as I do that things aren't the same anymore," Da-ae mimicked Jaeyun's words. What did he mean, things weren't the same? He was the only one who wasn't the same anymore. She had been the same since the beginning. She hated all the happy couples who had passed by them that day, and she hated Jaeyun. She was startled to see that she had so much hatred and negativity lurking within her. But soon, it ceased to matter. Da-ae bit her lip. It tasted bitter and bloody.

Was Jaeyun crying in the restroom? Was he hurting, too? Did he feel bad? Or was he relieved? Da-ae held back all the questions and thoughts crowding her mind. Keeping her thoughts to herself was what she did best. Perhaps it was her ability to do so that had kept her out of danger and trouble throughout her life.

But how strange. She felt that on this day, she didn't have to do that. Or to be precise, she didn't want to. A strange atmosphere, different from usual, was surrounding her.

"Arrrgh!"

Someone screamed. Da-ae thought that she herself had screamed. It was a relief, actually. *I guess my nerves have snapped,* she thought to herself as she sank to the ground, ready to give up. Again, someone let out a piercing scream. It wasn't Da-ae's low scream, or the sound of people on rides shouting in excitement.

People crowded over to see who was screaming. Something was wrong. Da-ae made her way slowly to the commotion, as if possessed. The nearer she got, the more humid the air felt, and a strange sickening feeling enveloped her.

She arrived at the edge of the crowd that was surrounding something. The people, who had been standing in a circle, scattered away screaming all at once. They ruthlessly shoved past her. Da-ae got pushed further back. Something was happening up ahead. Da-ae felt that she had to see what was going on with her own eyes. She felt as though she could hear a raspy voice echoing deep from a cave.

Go see for yourself. See what's happening with your own eyes.

Da-ae pushed her way through the people who were fleeing

and shoving past her, and reached the center. There was something curled up on the ground. Da-ae looked right at the thing before her eyes.

It was a huge lump that appeared to be wet and sticky. It looked like a piece of gum that a giant had chewed up and spat out, and also like an enormous, underdeveloped fetus. The lump moved in small motions. It seemed like a living organ as it stirred from time to time. On top of the large lump was a relatively small lump, clinging like a leech. The two took turns expanding and contracting, as if they were breathing. There was no sound of screaming now.

Da-ae took another step forward. As she did, a sweet smell pierced her nose, making her feel dizzy. She had never smelled anything so overwhelmingly sweet before. She felt dazed, as if she were on drugs. She held her nose and rubbed her eyes, trying to see clearly. Narrowing her eyes, she looked once again at the lump in front of her.

It was jelly. Or rather, jelly that used to be people. A grown-up woman and a little child, intertwined, were melting away. They looked as though they were hugging each other tight.

"They'll never split up," Da-ae mumbled quietly.

She wondered if two people would melt away like that if they jumped into lava while hugging each other. She pictured herself and Jaeyun jumping into a pit of fire together.

The sticky, transparent surface soon provided a clear view of the nerves, organs, and bones becoming mashed together. The lump had now melted into a pool on the ground and was spreading wider and wider. There was a yellow outfit on top of a blue dress.

Da-ae raised her head and looked around. The crowd was long gone by now. The only person who remained was a little girl, who for some time had been unable to take her eyes off the lump. Clutching her backpack straps and looking as pale as death, the girl mumbled to herself, "It's all because of the jelly …"

Da-ae looked at the girl's trembling hands. Then she glanced down at her bag. The packet of jelly, which she hadn't been able to share with Jaeyun in the end, was completely crumpled up.

"This jelly will keep you from ever breaking up. It's magic jelly. You'll be inseparable for the rest of your life, I promise," she recalled the man saying as he handed her the packet. Instantly, her eyes began to shine.

"Oh!" Da-ae exclaimed. She broke into a radiant smile, which chased away the dark shadows on her face. Looking like a believer who had finally realized the truth, she pulled out the packet of jelly from her bag.

She began to run with the packet in her hand. She felt relieved, as though she had found the solution to a problem she hadn't been able to solve for a long time. The fish bone that had been stuck in her throat, stopping her from making a sound, melted softly, and slid down her throat like jelly. Each time she breathed in, a sweet smell tickled her nose and airway. She felt certain that if the particles in the air could be magnified at that moment, they would be pink.

Da-ae could talk again at last. She had something to say to Jaeyun. Dream Teddy was setting off firecrackers in her head. She ran, feeling the sparks descending into her heart and mind. Her heart was so light that she felt like she could fly. Her face was full of exhilaration. With each energetic step she took came the sound of people screaming from everywhere, as if her feet were pressing a button. The people began to melt away, each making a different sound. Cold drops of liquid fell onto Da-ae's face.

Sticky rain was pouring down. Da-ae stopped running and stood at a corner. She wiped away what was on her face with her palm. She saw that it was a deep pink slime. She looked up at the sky.

The Drop Tower had stopped at the top. It showed no signs of coming down, just like Da-ae's heightened mood. Several more drops of pink slime fell onto her face. A damp breeze scattered her hair.

Da-ae wiped roughly at her face. She closed her eyes for a moment and heard something splashing, like the sound of water balloons exploding. She opened her eyes slowly. The wind brought with it squishy arms and legs which fell like rain. Da-ae stared blankly at the limbs that fell from the sky and squashed like pudding against the ground. Covering her head, she began to run again. She ran, looking straight ahead, amid the festival-like sounds of people screaming and bodies exploding like firecrackers.

Da-ae was standing in front of a mushroom-shaped restroom. From inside, she heard the sound of water running. She stood there in front of the translucent door, catching her breath. Her face was flushed red, as though she were drunk from breathing in the sweet smell. She put her hands on her cheeks and felt how hot they were. Her heart fluttered, just like it had the first time she talked to Jaeyun.

Da-ae looked into the small mirror hanging in front of the

restroom. Her long hair was a mess, with chunks of pink jelly sticking to it. She tried to comb her hair with her hand, but like chewed-up gum, the jelly didn't come off easily. At that moment, she heard someone moving inside. She cautiously put her hand on the doorknob. Her fingers were trembling slightly. She pulled the door open and found Jaeyun inside. She gazed at his sweet, familiar face. His eyes were red. Looking at those eyes, wet with tears, Da-ae asked in a small voice—so small that it sounded as though she were talking to herself—"Were you crying?"

Jaeyun said nothing in reply. He seemed startled by her sudden appearance and the way she looked. His hands automatically reached out to touch her hair.

"What happened? What's all that in your hair?" he asked. His concerned voice was so tender that Da-ae couldn't believe he had just broken up with her. She closed her eyes, feeling the touch of his hand.

How can you say you don't love me when you're so worried about me? Da-ae wondered. Her slowly opening eyelids revealed her pupils. She raised her hand and touched his cheek. With an awkward look on his face, Jaeyun grasped her wrist and pulled it down.

"We can't ..." he began.

We can't, what? What are you saying? Da-ae asked in her mind. Her eyes had lost their focus but became sharp all of a sudden. Jaeyun didn't have a chance to finish what he was saying. Da-ae grabbed him by the back of his head and stuffed his mouth with a handful of jelly she had been holding.

"Eat it, eat it!" she screamed, her teeth clenched. She covered his mouth so that he couldn't spit out the jelly. In the confusion of the moment, Jaeyun swallowed the jelly, which he had barely even chewed. Da-ae saw his throat move as he swallowed. She laughed, her face contorted. Her fingers went limp.

Bewildered, Jaeyun finally managed to shove her away. She didn't cling to him. A peaceful smile rose to her lips. Coughing, Jaeyun spat out what remained in his mouth.

Glaring at Da-ae, he shouted, "What are you doing?"

"Let's not break up. Let's stay together forever," Da-ae said in a singsong voice.

"Are you crazy?" Jaeyun said and ran out of the restroom, gasping for breath. He stepped on something sticky. The strange sensation made him stop and look around. Everywhere around him was a pool of mysterious pink slime. An unpleasant, sweet odor had been tickling his nose for a while now. He heard people screaming somewhere.

Plop! Plop! Drops of heavy liquid fell onto his face. He wiped his face with his hands and saw that they were covered in a translucent and sticky, pink slime. He looked up at the sky. Something resembling pink syrup was trickling down from the Drop Tower, which had stopped at the top.

He then felt all his senses going numb. He felt heavy and suffocated, as though he were moving underwater. Something made him look at his hands; he saw that all ten of his fingers were gone. They had melted into the same pink slime that was on his face.

Jaeyun let out a shriek. From behind him came the sound of Da-ae laughing merrily away. He wanted to turn his head but he couldn't move as he wished. He couldn't budge, as though he were paralyzed. He saw his reflection in the window across from him. His skin was melting.

Da-ae jumped to her feet and went up to Jaeyun, who was screaming. His voice grew fainter and fainter as his vocal cords melted away. Drops of slime scattered into the air as he flailed his arms around. Looking excited, Da-ae grasped his face. Something mushy oozed out from between her fingers. It felt like thickening jam. Her voice elated, she said the words she had been dying to say the whole time she was running over to him: "This is our first day together, all over again ..."

Jaeyun's features were all but gone now. Da-ae put her mouth to the hole that probably used to be his mouth and tasted something so sweet that it burned her tongue. A squishy lump of jelly came off him and slid down her throat. A strange fever spread out from within her heart.

Da-ae leaned fully into Jaeyun, who was standing still. Her lips mashing into the wet, sticky lump, she put her arms around his waist. She felt as though she were hugging a huge pudding. Her fingers began to slowly melt away. She smiled. As her vision became more and more blurred, she gazed happily at herself and Jaeyun becoming one.

Two Hundred Meters to the Hamster Wheel

I was born in a rural town on the outskirts of Seoul. To get to school, I had to ride a bus which came only once an hour for about thirty minutes. My mom ran a small eatery in town. We didn't have many customers. Even now, I don't think my mom's food is particularly good. Our main source of income was the money that my dad, who had left home, sent us every once in a while.

The image that comes to mind when I think of my childhood is that of my mom hunkered down in her room counting money. She didn't bother to hide the fact that we were poor. She was probably so tired that she had no energy to make the effort to do so. I tried to understand her, even though she didn't acknowledge my efforts.

My mom was all I had—she was the only one I had in the world to love and the only one I had to resent. During my adolescence, I resented her for making me come into the world. I hated her more than I hated the bullies who harassed me at school and even more than the teacher who played favorites. I wanted to go to Seoul. I thought things would work out somehow if only I went to Seoul. There were so many things in Seoul that couldn't be found in a rural town. So I left home as soon as I graduated from high school. My mom didn't try to stop me.

It wasn't that I wanted to go to college. I didn't have the money for it anyway. I was overwhelmed enough just trying to get by in Seoul. I went to Seoul to make money, solely to make money. I wanted to make money somehow, make a lot of money, and … what did I want to do with the money?

Jua's little head wobbled from side to side. Pulling at my fingers, she let out a cheer. A wide-eyed bear was handing out balloons in front of the carousel. Jua's eyes sparkled as she stared at the balloons. I gave her back a gentle push.

"Go on and get one," I told her.

"Okay!" came the eager reply, and she sprinted off as though she had just been waiting for my permission.

The bear, walking with its hips swaying, handed her a balloon with a character printed on it. She came running back with the balloon in her hand and threw herself into my arms. I loved feeling her softness. Suddenly, Jua pointed a short finger at my head.

"Mom, can I have that hairpin?" she asked.

"What hairpin?" I asked, and felt my head; I found something hard over my ponytail.

"Oh, this," I said.

It was an acrylic hairpin in the shape of a conch—the only one of my mother's belongings I had taken with me when I left home. I was a bit hesitant at first, but in the end, I took it out of my hair and put it in Jua's. Jua cried easily and was very stubborn, so when there was something she wanted, the easiest thing was to let her have it. She seemed very happy with the pin in her hair. Humming a song and looking at her reflection in a window, she twirled around and around, like the mascot dancing and twirling up ahead.

I have never really thought that Jua takes after me. I mean she does look a little like me since she's my daughter, but she takes more after her dad, if anything. But today, with my mom's hairpin in her hair, she looked uncannily like me when I was young. But I had no memories of good times at a theme park. The only good memory I had was of playing with my cat in the yard.

We had a cat when I was young. My mom had brought home a kitten that had been quietly hanging around her store. The kitten, abandoned by her own mother, became quite attached to my mom, as though she were her mother. She was a tuxedo cat with yellow eyes, and looked as though she came right out of a cartoon. Her four paws were white, as if she was wearing boots, and my mom would often hold one of her paws and shake it, as though the cat was a human child. My mom always looked tired but brightened up in those moments. She loved the cat so much that sometimes I felt jealous.

I liked the cat, too. I remember how I used to laugh after putting my mom's hairpin on her head. The cat would walk around looking annoyed, the hairpin dangling from her head. After a day or so I would find the hairpin somewhere in the house, and I would pick it up and put it in my own hair. The house was always full of cat hair.

My mom passed away long ago from an illness. She died not even knowing what illness she had because she never went to the hospital. All this happened before this theme park opened. New Seoul Park was built where the brick house I lived in used to be.

Once, I dropped by the house before it was about to be torn down. There was no one and nothing there. I wondered where the cat had gone. She had probably died, since cats have a very short lifespan compared to humans. The thought made me envy the cat. The cat probably had my mom by its side when it died, but my mom had no one there when she died. My mom had no one but me, but I wasn't at her side, so she probably had died alone.

Jua pointed somewhere with her finger. It was a sign that read, 200 METERS TO THE HAMSTER WHEEL.

"I want to go on that ride!" Jua exclaimed.

"Walk slowly and be careful not to fall," I said.

Completely ignoring my words, Jua darted toward the wheel. I shouted, telling her to be careful, but she didn't seem to hear me. The heat had drained me of energy, so I walked, following her with my eyes. It was strange how there weren't that many people in just that corner of the park. But thanks to that, I didn't have to worry about Jua getting lost in a crowd.

I walked up the hill after Jua, who was running lightly up. But she came back down in a moment, looking disappointed. She tugged at my sleeve and said, "The wheel is under repair. And a strange man said he wanted to give me some jelly, so I just came back down."

"Nothing happened, right?" I asked.

She nodded. My heart dropped at the thought that she could have fallen victim to a criminal targeting children. After checking to make sure that there was nothing wrong with her, I turned around and we headed in another direction. We rode the carousel and a few other kids' rides, then went to sit on a bench. I was thirsty so I sipped on a sports drink I had brought from home. I offered Jua some, but she shook her head, saying, "I just get thirstier when I drink something lukewarm."

She sat there for a while swinging her legs. Then her eyes focused on something. A girl around Jua's age was walking past us, carrying a stuffed Dream Teddy the size of her own body, and a cold drink with water droplets beaded on the outside in her other hand. Jua followed her persistently with her eyes until the girl had disappeared into a dot. I almost let out a little sigh but managed to hold it back. I knew what Jua wanted without her telling me. Looking at my face, she began to open her mouth to say something. Soon, the words I had dreaded popped out of her mouth.

"Dream Teddy is humongous."

"He sure is."

"I wish I had a big teddy bear like that, too. Then I wouldn't get bored even when you go to work."

Nodding my head, I tried to guess how much the bear would cost. A palm-sized stuffed animal usually cost about fifteen-thousand won. A child-sized bear probably cost at least seventy-thousand won, possibly much more. The thought made me break into a cold sweat. We had been able to come to the theme park thanks to the tickets someone at work had given me, but my budget was too tight to let Jua enjoy anything extra. I had already spent more money than I had planned on transportation and on food that hadn't even tasted good, though it had looked pretty. I chewed lightly on my lip.

I had expected that she would want a toy. There was always something or other that she wanted. Still, I had wanted to bring her to the theme park because I didn't want her to have a bleak childhood. I wanted the past to shine brightly for Jua when she remembered it in the future. That was something I had wanted for myself all my life but hadn't been able to have.

When there was something she wanted, I always made sure that she got it, even if it meant that I had to go out of my way to do so. I was happy to buy her what she wanted. I felt like a good, capable mother, thoughtful and attentive. In doing so, however, I had overlooked the fact that the older children get, the more things they want. Once again, I did the math in my head to calculate the remaining expenses for the month. Just last week for her friend's birthday party, I had bought Jua an expensive outfit as well as a gift for the friend. A stuffed animal that big was simply out of the question. I put a hand on Jua's shoulder, and smiling, I said, "Jua, a teddy bear that big is hard to play with and to wash. Why don't we get a small one?"

"I already have a small one at home. I like the big one. Get me the big one, Mom, please?"

"You have so many stuffed animals at home, though. It would be a waste of money."

"But I want it! I want it!" she demanded, shouting.

I sensed people staring at us as they passed. I tried to appease her, making an attempt to keep myself from frowning. Tears began to flow from her eyes. I felt a dull ache in my heart. I had made a real effort to bring her to the park—I had been willing to dip pretty deep into the monthly budget.

When I was young, I had always pestered my mom whenever

we went grocery shopping in town. I asked for things I knew I couldn't have. I wanted her to feel guilty and hated her for not being able to give me what I wanted. Now, I could understand the chill that came into her eyes whenever I had made such demands.

I pulled Jua by her wrist. She wouldn't budge from the bench. I let out a deep sigh. Again, I looked her in the eyes and urged, "Jua, are you going to listen to me or not?"

"I want a teddy bear! I want one! Is it because we're poor that we can't buy one?"

"What do you mean?"

"Kids make fun of me. They say I'm poor because I don't have a dad."

I didn't know what to say. Opening and closing her little fists, she said in a tearful voice, "You're always out working, and I have nothing to play with at home. Some of my friends even have cell phones, but I ..."

Jua glared at me, her tearful face scrunched up. She looked like a little devil. I was the one who wanted to cry here.

"If you keep this up, I'm going to leave you here," I said firmly, trying not to get choked up.

Jua didn't say anything. Pouting, she still wouldn't budge from her spot. I heaved a big sigh, loudly on purpose, and turned around. I began to stomp away. Normally, she would start following me reluctantly by this point, but today, she showed no sign of doing so. She was still sitting on the bench. What had gotten into her? She was increasingly turning into a stubborn crybaby, it seemed.

"This is the last time I'm going to say this. If you don't come with me now, I'm going to leave you here for real," I said.

Jua trembled slightly but turned her head away. I walked straight ahead with Jua behind me. I don't know how long I walked. I felt faint from the heat of the blazing sun. With my hands on my forehead and feverish from the heat, I sat hunched on the ground. A few people passing by asked me if I was all right, but I just shook my head. I wasn't all right.

Where had it all gone wrong? When I was young, I had wanted to be able to give my future children everything they ever wanted. I resolved that if I couldn't do that, I wouldn't have a child in the first place. I started earning money early on and took night classes at a university even though it wasn't easy. I met my husband when I was earning enough to make ends meet. He was a researcher on his way to becoming a university professor, and I thought he was my chance. Our marriage wasn't something that had just happened without a plan.

My husband became a professor not long after Jua was born—not a full-time professor, but a part-time lecturer. Things were okay when he was working both as a researcher and a lecturer. He was always saying that he had good connections and would go on to become a full-time professor in no time. I took his word for it. Then he quit his research post and began to follow around those "connections." That was when things began to rapidly deteriorate. I had to find a job because he no longer had an income. I had to start all over from the beginning because my previous work experience didn't count.

My husband became more and more unhinged. He brought home old books, saying they would help him in his effort to become a professor, and stayed cooped up in his room; he never came out and turned into a complete shut-in. I tried to drag him out by force, but it didn't work. I didn't know what he did in there, but there were always ants swarming around the room and it stank. A ton of packages piled up by the door almost every day. All of the packages contained jelly.

The day his eyes lost focus completely, I ran from the old apartment with Jua. I can't forget the feel of his hand on my shoulder as he tried to stop me. It was unbelievably soft and limp, and horribly clammy. I never saw him again after that. Where could he have gone? Oh, everything is so tangled up—like a knotted ball of thread that can never be unraveled.

The afternoon sun burned the top of my head. I pictured Jua's head wobbling from side to side. I raised my head and looked at my hands, which had been wrapped around my head. My fingers were awfully thin; when had I lost so much weight? I saw an overlapping image of my mom's fingers—fingers I had held a very long time ago.

It was as hot and stifling that day as it was today. It was decades ago but somehow, I could recall the moment with clarity. I had let go of my mom's hand, which I had been holding tightly, as a bustling crowd had pushed past me. No, actually, I hadn't. Her fingers had slipped out of my hand. I remember how they felt as they easily freed themselves from my grip. They fluttered for a second like a fish in a child's hand, then slipped away.

After roaming around the market for a long time, I was able to go home with the help of someone I knew. My mom was home but she didn't say anything to me. I could never bring myself to ask her how she had lost her hold on my hand, or if she had simply let go of it. Now I could guess what she would have said, had I asked.

I ran my bony hand over my face. It felt damp. I got up and began to run toward the bench where I had left Jua. It was still noisy all around. Soon I saw the bench where we had sat. Jua, who should have been sitting there like a good child, was nowhere to be seen. There was no one and nothing there.

"Jua? Jua!" I called out at the top of my voice. It felt like the world was spinning around me. I asked everyone who passed by if they had seen Jua, but no one had. I saw an employee in a green uniform nearby. I dragged my shaking body over to him and demanded, "A girl in a yellow T-shirt. Oh, and she's wearing a purple hairpin that looks like a conch. Have you seen her?"

The employee, with a yellow-green hat jammed deep down on his head, pointed somewhere. His finger was pointing at the sign that said 200 METERS TO THE HAMSTER WHEEL. I ran at once. With each step up the hill, I got more out of breath. There were a lot more people there now than there had been earlier. I kept calling out Jua's name. But no one turned around to even look at me, even though I was shouting so loudly. It was as if people couldn't hear me. I looked and looked, pushing my way through the crowd. Every time I put my hand on someone's shoulder, they vanished like a mirage. I couldn't seem to be able to get a hold of anything.

I stood among the people passing by, calling out to Jua at the top of my lungs. I sensed something odd but couldn't afford to get distracted by anything. Then I saw some familiar figures: a mother and a daughter walking through a crowd, holding hands. The woman, her hair pinned up with a conch-shaped hairpin, looked weary with exhaustion, and the little girl was expressionless, her face devoid of any childlike innocence. Only then did I realize that I was in the town where I had lost my mom, not in the theme park. I followed after the mother and daughter. Replaying before my eyes was the moment I had so wanted to forget.

As we crossed the intersection, a group of drunk hikers came thronging in. The woman glanced down at the girl. As the girl shifted a little to the side so as not to bump into the crowd, the woman broke free of her hand and got lost in the crowd of hikers.

Left alone, the girl stood there for a long time, staring down at her empty hand. She then raised her head. My young self was looking at me. I took one step, then another, toward myself. I had to take myself home. But no matter how much I walked, the distance between us remained the same. My young self was still looking at me with a piercing gaze. On the verge of tears, I extended my arms. The face of my young self became blurry, like when different colors of paint are mixed together with a paintbrush, and before I knew it, Jua was standing there. I called out her name.

When I opened my eyes, I saw a ceiling with a pretty pattern and a signboard that read INFIRMARY. A nurse sitting by my side asked me if I was awake and went on to say, "You passed out on the road to the Hamster Wheel. Luckily, there's nothing seriously wrong with you—you probably just strained yourself in the heat. You'll be all right after a good rest. Did you have anyone with you?"

I felt like I had just had a terrible nightmare but couldn't remember what it was about. At her words, I sat up and looked around quickly. I asked the flustered nurse, "What about my daughter? Wasn't there a girl around me, about nine years old?"

"You were alone when you passed out ... If you've lost your child, I'll call the Lost Children Center. You'll be able to find her soon. It usually takes less than half an hour," the nurse said.

Immediately, I rushed out of the infirmary. I went into the red mushroom-shaped house that had the words LOST CHILDREN CENTER written on it and gave the employees a description of Jua. They looked around, and one of them said with a nervous look on his face, "Uh, she was just here, right over there with another girl her age ... maybe they went to the bathroom?"

I was so distraught that I didn't even get angry. One thing was for sure, though: Jua had been fine when she was at the Lost Children Center. She had been there just moments before, so she couldn't have gone far. I came out of the center and began looking around the park again.

To my great relief, I found her not too far away. She was sitting on a bench in the distance, swinging her legs. I felt as though my legs would give out under me, but I managed to stay on my feet.

"Jua!" I cried out.

I ran to her as fast as I could. Her eyes slowly turned to me. My own face—the face of the little girl at the intersection—overlapped with hers. I would never be separated from her again. I would never let go of her hand again. I hugged her tightly to my chest.

The Sabbath

Director Yu Hyeongyeong pulled down the stifling mask that covered more than half of her face. She felt refreshed for a second, but then the sharp, pungent smell of disinfectant penetrated her nose, making her grimace. The nasty smell intensified as she breathed in. She felt as though the olfactory cells in her nose would melt away.

She had been scouring three whole floors of the building with bleach since sunrise, so the awful smell was inevitable. She calmly straightened herself, wiping the frown off her face. Soon back to her serene self, she looked into the eyes of her staff standing in four straight rows.

"Thank you all for your work today!" she said.

"Thank you!" the staff replied, applauding.

After watching them get on the shuttle bus one by one, Hyeongyeong headed to her car. The stench grew worse and worse instead of fading away, giving her a headache. Irritated, she reached out a hand and fumbled through the glove compartment. The compartment was full of little packets of jelly that were sold in large quantities. She pulled one out, tore it open, and chewed on a piece of jelly, savoring its sweetness. The smell of disinfectant gradually diminished.

In the distance, she saw the huge shuttle bus making its way out of the parking lot. Hyeongyeong turned on the ignition of her car. On the side of the bus was a picture of herself smiling, holding a blue-green spray bottle of bleach, along with the name of her company, "Gwangnan Cleaning." Feeling half proud and half embarrassed, she stared at the large picture of her face on the bus. She finally left the parking lot, driving slowly, when the bus disappeared from view. She was planning on taking a little nap before going out to give a guest lecture at a university in the afternoon.

Ever since her name made a business paper's list of outstanding CEOs the year before, Hyeongyeong had been invited from time to time to give lectures, both small and large. Her company had made headlines for providing proper benefits to its employees, which was rare in the cleaning service industry. One of the employees had posted a story on social media about how the head of the company worked alongside the staff every morning, and people treated her like a saint for taking part in the difficult work. Someone had even taken a picture of her wearing a mask, which had led to a barrage of interview requests.

"Cleaning in the morning is a sort of spiritual practice for me. Most people consider cleaning to be simple labor, but the labor is a religious cleansing ritual of sorts in that it purifies what's been contaminated. As I work and sweat with my staff every morning, I'm taking part in a spiritual ceremony. It's not an act of service, nor is it a tool for me to manage my image and reputation; it's simply something I do to strengthen myself."

The New Seoul Park Jelly Massacre

That was the answer Hyeongyeong had given to the aggressive question, "Isn't early morning cleaning something you do just for your business's image?" And her words, captured along with scenes from her lectures, floated around the internet with titles such as "a-typical-entrepreneur-in-korea.jpg" and "a CEO who gets 200% satisfaction out of her job." Some of her employees even came up to her and asked for an autograph for their kids. "My kids say they want to be like you," they would say. Then Hyeongyeong would smile enigmatically and say, "They need to be smarter than me."

Back home now, Hyeongyeong stood by the front door with her eyes closed and her hands clasped together. She looked as devout as a monk as she recited something that sounded like a chant or a prayer. She opened her eyes slowly after a moment and took a look around. The apartment looked as clean as new, just as it had been before she had left. Hyeongyeong had mysophobia, which meant that there was no dust in this apartment. Even spots that were easy to overlook—the top of the refrigerator, window frames, tea cabinet shelves, and so on—had a sheen to them, and neither were there things like mold or even water stains that could easily be found in other homes.

Smiling in satisfaction, Hyeongyeong went into her room. She took her suit jacket off and poured herself a glass of wine, then walked over to a door. The secret room, which had been created by tearing down the walls between the bathroom and walk-in closet, along with the storage room, could only be entered with a scan of her fingerprint.

Hyeongyeong took a sip of wine and put her finger on the

locking device. The door opened with a simple beep. There were no windows in the room, meaning that it was as dark as night despite it being midday. She flicked on the light switch and a reddish light dimly illuminated the curious objects placed around the room.

There was the hand of a mummy, though there was no telling if it was real or fake; a stone statue of the devil; an upside-down crucifix; and voodoo dolls commonly used in cursing rituals. Hyeongyeong had devoted herself to collecting these items. She had gone to great trouble to smuggle some of them from Africa and other far-flung corners of the world.

Hyeongyeong walked past her prized possessions to the end of the room. Among all her cherished artifacts, there was one she held particularly dear. Placed on an art-nouveau display cabinet at least a century old was a single book. Hyeongyeong placed her glass down and put on cotton gloves over her rough hands. She reached out a hand and carefully pulled out the old book. When she opened the blank cover, a faded yellow page appeared. In a low voice, she read the sentence written on the first page.

"We dance with the devil."

Hyeongyeong's face, illuminated by the red light, seemed to sway strangely. She closed the book and sat down at a desk with a laptop on it. As she turned on the laptop, a picture appeared on the dark screen. It was an engraving that showed the devil, as well as some devil worshipers performing a ritual. The engraving, created by an anonymous artist from the Middle Ages, was among Hyeongyeong's collections. The artist, too, must have belonged to the group of worshipers.

Hyeongyeong clicked on the engraving, and the cauldron in the picture began to boil, and the hand protruding from the cauldron began to melt. After the simple animation ended, a message board appeared on the screen. Hyeongyeong saw the post at the top. It was written by someone named Sodok, meaning disinfection—Hyeongyeong's nickname. The post, which she had written the day before, had gotten a lot of attention and comments and was pinned to the top of the board as the most popular post of the day. She clicked on it.

THE SABBATH WILL COME

Our ancestors were those who couldn't make it to the top of anything socio-economically. *He* took them into His embrace and watched over them. These ancestors gave up their religion, country, and family, and became His servants of their own free will. And they survived. We witches are everywhere. He is no illusion. He does exist. I am proof of that. I have His book and can read His writing. I have seen Him face to face.

He soothes our hearts. He hands us sweet, sweet jelly in the moment of our greatest need. The day is on the horizon—the Sabbath is coming, no question about it. The day of the banquet is approaching. He is kind and merciful. Only faith will lead us to the Sabbath.

It seems, however, that a few of you are impatient and are making rash speculations about, and misunderstanding, His intentions. There's no use trying to guess where the Sabbath will be held. That's not important—only those who are chosen can take part in the banquet. Expending energy on futile efforts will only put you out of favor with Him. I hope you all have a good day.

Reading all the comments on her posts was probably Hyeongyeong's one and only hobby. Low-ranking members uploaded several posts a day on their speculations about the true identity of Sodok, a prominent member of the online community.

Whenever she saw those posts, full of baseless speculations stating that she was a renowned professor of liberal arts, or a business tycoon who probably owned the hotel that was in one of her pictures, or a criminal who used to be a pseudo-religious fanatic, Hyeongyeong felt quite pleased. She felt as though she were their god or something—someone who could be anyone, but in fact, was no one. That was Sodok. With a light heart she went on reading all the comments of praise and agreement. Then, she came across a sentence that aggravated her:

"You've got it all wrong."

The user's nickname was Jelly Bean. Hyeongyeong bit her lip. He was the only one on this dark web website who got on her nerves. He nitpicked at everything she wrote, posting counterarguments and picking fights. The other users, who at first thought he was just a troll, were beginning to consider him Sodok's rival as he tirelessly went on contradicting her.

"Rival? Yeah, right," Hyeongyeong muttered.

She couldn't tolerate him. She had to be the first in rank, at least in this group of people who worshiped Him. Why? Because she had heard His voice; she had seen Him face to face; she had His book. And she could read it. There had to be only one person in the world—herself—who could do that; if not, it would all be meaningless.

She clicked off the post and saw a post with a shining icon that said "new."

"The Sabbath is coming to New Seoul Park—argument against Sodok's assertion," read the title.

The new post quickly rose to the top, moving up past Hyeongyeong's post. It was written by Jelly Bean. Hyeongyeong's face screwed up into a scowl. She knew what the post would say. "We have the right to be chosen by Him because we believe in and worship Him. We must bring about the Sabbath." That sort of crap.

It was all useless. He wasn't someone that mere humans could comprehend. But He was merciful—He would come if they waited, each doing their part. But Jelly Bean was much too insolent, especially for someone who supposedly worshiped Him. So what if Jelly Bean could find out beforehand where He would appear, where the Sabbath would take place? Did he think he could be the one to usher in the day? "He's challenging me," Hyeongyeong muttered to herself in a low voice.

Even more ridiculous were some of the comments. Several people had posted words of praise for Jelly Bean, denouncing Hyeongyeong and Him in an aggressive tone. It was blasphemy. Her eyes burned and her grip on the mouse tightened. She didn't truly care what Jelly Bean had been doing or thinking thus far, but this time, she could not turn a blind eye. She put a hand on her forehead and calmed herself down.

Jelly Bean. Who was he? He was rude, to be sure, but his

earlier posts on various analyses and interpretations of rare books had been quite impressive. Hyeongyeong's guess was that *he* was a professor, with a university research lab all to himself—she could tell from his arrogant attitude. He probably always did as he pleased, acting like the king of the world, with the future of graduate students in his hands.

Hyeongyeong had reached her limit. Jelly Bean's new post was proof that he was a traitor. The smell of disinfectant stung her nose. She knew that the smell wasn't real and that it wouldn't disappear even if she held her nose.

She felt a headache coming on. She closed her eyes and fingered a corner of the book, which was covered in worn-out leather. In the darkness, memories from the past flashed through her mind like an afterimage. How foolish and ignorant she had been until she had received Him. But there are no meaningless coincidences. Every coincidence is like a stitch in a piece of crossstitch embroidery. This, too, must be a part of His design.

*

Looking back now on the early days of her marriage, Hyeongyeong realized that it had been nothing short of a comedy. Her husband had been as proud and arrogant as could be, and her mother-in-law, who believed that there was no one in the world better than her son, had treated her daughter-in-law like a slave. All the education her mother-in-law had received, and her post as a university professor, and still she acted this way toward Hyeongyeong. What Hyeongyeong found laughable now was that she herself had been no different from them. Why had she been so terrified of a stubborn old woman? And with all these characters who all had a screw loose, what could her life be other than a comedy?

Gang Panju, her mother-in-law, had a serious case of mysophobia. Even if Hyeongyeong cleaned the house, her mother-in-law would make a fuss about it being filthy. There were times when Hyeongyeong had to mop and mop until her fingers bled. At the time, rather than getting upset, Hyeongyeong had pitied her mother-in-law, telling herself that the woman was mentally ill. Graciously, Hyeongyeong did as she was told, thinking she would humor her mother-in-law since the woman probably didn't have many days left to live anyway.

It was laughable indeed—who was she to pity the woman, when she herself was the one in need of pity? Only after a long time had passed, after all ten of her fingers had become torn and cracked and swollen, did Hyeongyeong realize that Panju had never suffered from mysophobia. The woman had simply acted out of malice.

By the time the truth dawned on her, Hyeongyeong had reached a point where she couldn't keep herself from all the mopping. She was the one who had mysophobia now, not her mother-in-law. Hyeongyeong could not leave a single speck of dust or stain unattended. Her fingers became more and more worn out, and the smell of disinfectant always lingered around her nose.

The only way to rid herself of the smell, which seemed to paralyze her senses, was to keep something very sweet in her mouth. Hyeongyeong always had something sweet in her mouth, things her husband wouldn't even touch, saying they left a bad aftertaste. She had cavities because of them, but she couldn't give them up.

She had even less to say about her husband. He was completely incapable of doing anything. And yet he had started a business—a cleaning service in association with a patented bleach product. Since the business was in its early stage, there was a lot of work and not enough people.

During the day, Hyeongyeong helped her husband out at work, and in the evening, she cleaned the apartment. She was always swamped with work. Her husband would get things started, but it was always up to her to work things out. Everyone wanted to discuss matters with her, not her husband, despite the fact that he was the head of the company. Hyeongyeong didn't even have a proper position, though. She got tired of people calling her "Ma'am" at work. She wanted to be called by a proper title and not have people refer to her as "the director's wife."

The way her mother-in-law treated her didn't change just because she had started working. On the contrary, she often hurled curses at Hyeongyeong, telling her not to let things get to her head. Her husband wasn't even at home most of the time—he came home drunk more than half of the week, and when he wasn't drunk, he came home late for no reason. Hyeongyeong wondered every night where on earth he could be. What was he doing, leaving her with all the work he should be handling himself? She felt a strange sensation in her stomach, as though there was a hot lump moving around inside. She glared at the rag in her hand.

Oh, I wish I could get rid of them, she thought.

Mysophobia attacked her now from the inside, beyond things that could be seen with the eyes. Her husband and mother-in-law felt, to her, like stains on a clean, white floor.

More and more often, her husband stayed out overnight. Hyeongyeong had no idea what those meetings of his were about, when she was the one doing all the work. If she demanded that he tell her, he went running to his mother and told her everything that had been said during their quarrel. He took things out of context, ignoring all evidence as to what really took place, and made things up so as to make it seem that he was the victim. Hyeongyeong became the difficult wife who wasn't considerate of her husband. His lies were so brilliant that she almost admired him in those moments. He should've been a writer. Panju was his only reader and fan, and the part of the villain always fell to Hyeongyeong.

After realizing how unreasonable they were, Hyeongyeong gave up trying to talk to them. She felt abandoned by the world and didn't feel like she would ever have a chance at a decent life again. She thought that she had made a wrong choice that had turned her life into hell and that she was being punished for it. It was unfair. She desperately needed a breakthrough.

She was grocery shopping one day when she noticed a small spice jar. She had several at home already, but she put it in her shopping basket on an impulse. When she got home, she filled the jar with the blue bleach she always used. The liquid sloshing around in the clear plastic jar looked quite pretty, like gems.

Hyeongyeong left the jar of bleach as it was for a long time. She needed time to prepare before putting her thoughts into action, even though what she had in mind wasn't anything extraordinary. Back then, she had been so nice and soft—too nice and soft, in fact. And above all, she needed a signal flare—a stimulus that would make her emotions, which were nearing the brim, rapidly escalate. The moment came so suddenly that it left her stupefied.

Panju, who had been humming all morning, seemed in a good mood that day. She didn't nag at Hyeongyeong even though she had quickly finished off a packet of jelly. The two had been eating together without Hyeongyeong's husband, who had gone out early the day before and hadn't come home yet, when Panju abruptly held out the paper.

"Director So-and-so, CEO of a Calmly Advancing Company."

So that was the best headline they could come up with for him. The photo showed Hyeongyeong's husband with a fake smile on his face. Hyeongyeong felt as if she was chewing on sand. She barely managed to swallow the food in her mouth before looking at Panju. The woman, now approaching her sixties, fingered the paper as though she found her son in the photo adorable. Repulsed, Hyeongyeong could only chuckle.

"How lucky you are to have him as your husband. Where would you find someone like him?" Panju said.

Thinking back, Hyeongyeong realized how constant Panju's love for her son had been. An entire wall of her room was covered with the awards her son, in his thirties at the time, had received since elementary school. To her, he himself was the greatest award, and her daughter-in-law was just a free gift that came with the award. The obvious fact finally hit home. Hyeongyeong swallowed the rice, which felt hard in her throat, and

The New Seoul Park Jelly Massacre

gulped down the nasty-smelling soup. She heard something snap inside her.

Three times a day, Hyeongyeong pulled out the spice jar that she kept hidden in a corner of the kitchen cabinet. Three times a day, she put a single drop of bleach in their food. She didn't think that what she was doing was insane. She was doing it just to feel a little better—like taking a vitamin pill after each meal.

She felt refreshed, as though she were chewing on a piece of mint gum, whenever she pictured the blue gem-like liquid, smelling of disinfectant, sliding down the throats of her husband and mother-in-law. She felt like she was slowly and carefully removing age-old stains. Three drops of bleach a day wouldn't do them any real harm. She was sure that the stress she was under had more of a detrimental impact on her body than the three drops of liquid had on theirs.

That day, a request for a special cleaning service had come in, which was rare. And as usual, Hyeongyeong's husband had gone off somewhere on the pretext of a meeting. In order to draw up the contract, someone had to go inspect the site and estimate the cost, so Hyeongyeong had been getting ready to travel since morning.

This kind of task actually belonged to the general manager, but he had come to Hyeongyeong for help after visiting the site, saying that it was impossible for him to estimate the cost. She wondered how bad it was—he certainly was making a great fuss. She sighed, thinking she was about to see something pretty ugly so early on in the day.

While her husband was guzzling booze with strangers in a dark basement bar in the middle of the day, Hyeongyeong was standing in front of an apartment building in the outskirts of Seoul that looked about ten years old. As she walked through the entrance of the building, the smell of stale humidity and dust tickled her nose. The elevator reeked of disinfectant. There was a mop and a bucket in the corner—someone must have been doing some cleaning. Hyeongyeong covered her nose and mouth with her hands. She suddenly began to worry that she might lose her sense of smell for good.

When she went up to the fourth floor, the landlady who had requested the service greeted her. The wealthy looking middle-aged woman, who seemed warm and genial, led Hyeongyeong to Room 407. A wave of unpleasant humidity rushed out as soon as the door opened. How could an apartment be so humid, when someone had been living in it? Something must have gone wrong during the construction. Hyeongyeong slowly stepped inside. A subtle, sweet smell grew stronger the further in she went, and it bothered her more than the humidity.

"It smells so funny in here—I wonder if they made candy here or something," the landlady said in a nasal voice.

There was a strange, eerie feeling inside the apartment. Hyeongyeong looked around the living room and the kitchen. Nothing really stood out to her. Same with the master bedroom. The people who had lived here must have left in a hurry as the covers on the bed had been left as they were. Hyeongyeong then headed toward another room further inside. This was the only door that was firmly shut in the apartment.

As she got closer to the room, an unfamiliar feeling washed

over her. Her mind felt clearer than usual, and she felt lighter. It was as though her brain cells, which had always been steeped in disinfectant, were awakening along with all her senses. She hadn't felt this cool and refreshed in a long time. She stood in front of the shut door.

The moment she put her hand on the doorknob and turned it, she realized the source of this refreshing feeling. An intensely sweet smell flooded out through the crack in the door. The smell of disinfectant that had so tortured her had been buried under the sweet smell inside.

Hyeongyeong opened her eyes wide and took a big breath through her nose and mouth. She didn't smell anything even slightly bitter, and she couldn't sense the smell of alcohol which had always irritated her nostrils. It was all sweetness. Her airways, which had seemed as though they would melt, felt clear now, and even the humidity, which was like a stickiness, felt pleasant to her.

The landlady, still holding her nose, went on to say, "The living room and the master bedroom are fine. I called you because of this little room. A couple lived here with their child. The woman was neat and clean, but the man was a bit odd. Then they all up and vanished the other night. I came to check on them because the rent hadn't come in, and this is what I found. They had already used up the security deposit to pay their rent in the past, so there was nothing left to give back."

Hyeongyeong stepped into the room in question, reveling in the sense of excitement in her heart. She caught a whiff of a heavy, sweet smell coming from beyond a wooden door covered in strange little marks. *Is this what diving into an enormous pudding feels like?* she wondered. She would have believed it if someone had told her that there were very fine particles of sugar in the air. Her nostrils tickled, and she sneezed several times in a row. With a hand over her mouth, she fumbled for a light switch on the wall. The light came on in the dark room. Finally managing to get her sneezing under control, she raised her head and looked straight ahead.

She had never seen anything like it before. The wallpaper was covered in indecipherable letters, and an entire wall was lined with old books. And more unusual than anything else was the great big lump, the size of an adult man and that was probably the cause of this humidity and sweet smell, that had been placed at the center of the room like an offering.

Slowly, Hyeongyeong approached the lump. She had seen something similar on a show that featured popular videos. The video was of someone playing with a clay-like lump called slime. The person would stretch it out and then mash the broken pieces back together. The lump would take on artificial colors, such as fluorescent green, pink, and sparkly gold. What was in front of Hyeongyeong looked exactly like that, a liquid monster—or slime, or jelly—that someone had played with roughly before discarding it. It was growing cold and hard as it gave off a sweet, artificial smell.

Hyeongyeong looked around the room. Everything in it looked suspicious, but it didn't particularly seem like the scene of a crime. Then something caught her eye, a book on a beat-up old desk. The book was so old that she was surprised anyone in this day and age would read something like that. The leather cover was tattered, and the pages were faded yellow. She casually flipped the book open but could not read it. The words were unintelligible.

The New Seoul Park Jelly Massacre

"So how much will it be, boss?" the landlady asked with her foot on the threshold, reluctant to go into the room herself.

Doing a quick estimation in her head, Hyeongyeong pulled out the contract and handed it to her, saying, "As you can see, this is an exceptional case. It would normally cost more, but we're offering a discount during our special sales event."

"Oh, whatever it takes. All I want is to get this place cleaned. I have trouble sleeping at night because of it."

"Then sign here, please. And I'd like to take a closer look at the room if that's all right."

"Sure," the landlady said, signing the contract at once as if to say there was nothing more to consider and handing Hyeongyeong the key.

Left to herself, Hyeongyeong examined the whole room. It would take a substantial amount of time and effort to clean the sticky slime that had splattered everywhere. It might even cost extra. Above all, she wasn't sure what to do with the gargantuan lump. Seeing how it smelled, she wondered if it should be handled as regular food waste. She could see why the general manager had tossed the job to her.

She was about to leave the room when the book she had placed back down on the desk tugged at her mind. She turned around and headed to the desk. She was overwhelmed by a strong urge to do so, as though someone were pushing her toward it. As she neared the desk, the book, which had been properly closed, spread open by itself. There was no wind, as there was no window inside the room. Mesmerized, Hyeongyeong watched what was happening. No one would believe her, but she felt that she was being given a divine revelation. It was as though something in the book was trying to talk to her. Her eyes fell on a sentence on one of the open pages.

We dance with the devil.

Finally, she put the book in her bag. It was strange how fast her heart was beating even though she wasn't stealing it, since everything in the room had to be cleaned out anyway. Once in a taxi, she took out the book and opened it again, but she still couldn't read it. Had its owner been able to read it? Where was he—or she—now?

She got out in front of her apartment complex. What an extraordinary day. The sun was grotesquely red as it went down the mountain behind the apartment buildings. Hyeongyeong was afraid—she felt as though blood would come pouring down from the sky. In the distance was her apartment, which would be under Panju's guard.

Hyeongyeong began to walk with heavy steps. She glanced at her cell phone, but her husband hadn't made a single call. He probably wasn't home. She would go home and eat dried-up, flavorless rice. She would put a drop of bleach as always into the rice bowl for her mother-in-law, who was nothing but a stain to her, then clean the floor with the same bleach. And then, and then ... what would happen then?

"Don't worry," said a stranger's voice from behind her.

Hyeongyeong whirled around. The taxi driver she'd thought had left already was standing there with the sun behind him. She couldn't see his face. Something about the man, as he stood there upright and erect, felt alien. He didn't seem to belong to this world.

"What did you say?" Hyeongyeong asked.

The New Seoul Park Jelly Massacre

He pointed to her bag with a stubby finger and said, "You'll be able to read it soon enough."

She could hear his voice, but his lips weren't moving. It was as if a mannequin was speaking.

Before she could ask him anything, he disappeared into the taxi. She rushed after the moving vehicle. As she waved her arms frantically, the taxi finally came to a stop. She banged on the window. The driver rolled it down and asked in irritation, "What do you want?"

"What did you just say?" Hyeongyeong asked.

"What? What's the matter with you?"

"You just said something to me back there!"

There was nothing of the mysterious air that had surrounded the man only moments before. He didn't seem to remember anything he had said. Hyeongyeong took her hands off the window. The taxi drove away and disappeared as soon as she pulled back. Had she really seen and heard what she thought she had? She headed home in a daze. With no one around, the apartment complex felt as empty as a cemetery.

When she opened the door to her apartment and entered, a deathly silence greeted her. The light wasn't even on in the living room. The only light in the dark apartment was the yellowish light coming from the kitchen.

"Mother," she called out, engulfed by an ominous feeling. She then saw Panju sitting at the table with her thin back to her. Her small body looked so black that Hyeongyeong wondered if what she was looking at was indeed a human being. Panju must have heard her come in, but she showed no response. She didn't even turn around. Hyeongyeong walked up to her slowly and carefully, like an explorer who had come across cursed remains. A delicious smell wafted in from the kitchen.

There was food laid out on the table. It was fried rice wrapped in a thin omelet. Steam was rising from the plate. How odd. Panju had never once prepared a meal for her. As Hyeongyeong reached out a hand to touch her mother-in-law's rigid shoulder, Panju finally opened her mouth. A hoarse voice came out, asking, "What is this?"

Panju was still looking straight ahead into thin air.

Hyeongyeong asked in a blank voice, "What do you mean, this?"

At last Panju turned her head to face her. The dull eyes, silently rolling this way and that, gave her the chills. Hyeongyeong thought she could hear a creaking sound with each movement Panju made, though she knew that wasn't actually the case. Panju's eyes were full of vehement emotion. Hyeongyeong stood there, frozen by her gaze.

Panju raised her wrist, thin and dry like a slice of beef jerky, and pointed toward the table. Her shriveled finger was pointing at a spice jar. It was Hyeongyeong's spice jar, with the gem-like blue liquid in it.

"Are you mad?" Panju asked, her voice as harsh as spoons scraping against a metal plate. Hyeongyeong's mind went blank.

"Ha ha …"

That was the sound of the bubbles inside her bursting. She recalled the massive lump she had seen that day. The bizarre atmosphere, the sweetish smell, and the severe humidity of that room began to engulf her. She laughed, her mind as clean and spotless as white fabric that had been washed with a ton of detergent and fabric softener. The bubbles would go out of her and leave their traces somewhere. Panju stared at her as though she was completely insane.

"Ha ha, ha ..."

Hyeongyeong couldn't stop laughing—she was like a deflating balloon. Her hand on her stomach, she stepped back slowly and sat down on the living room sofa. The floor seemed to be sinking. She was finally able to stop laughing. Panju came up to her. And then, and then ...

What did I do? But first ... what happened? Hyeongyeong wondered.

*

THE SABBATH IS COMING TO NEW SEOUL PARK—ARGUMENT AGAINST SODOK'S ASSERTION

So you think I'm making rash speculations and misinterpreting His intentions. You're wrong. The Sabbath is a kind of test for believers. It would lose its purpose if we don't figure out the answer through conjecture and analysis. And isn't it only natural to want to be near Him if you worship Him? The Sabbath is for us, not for Him, to bring about. Sodok claims to have met Him, but does she have proof? In my opinion, she either has paranoia or wants to monopolize what she has. If what she says is true, she should at least post a picture of the book's contents.

Oh, and one more thing: the Sabbath is coming to New Seoul Park, no doubt about it. You can figure that out by examining the intervals between the Sabbaths and the distinct characteristics of the areas in which they were held, and by studying the theory of divination based on topography. To tell the truth, I have the book too. It's all in the book. I'm not as selfish and petty as someone we all know.

Hyeongyeong had a hard time tearing herself away from Jelly Bean's words. The more she read them, the more ridiculous they seemed, but they were so audacious that she couldn't get over them. The last three sentences were clearly aimed at her. She took a sip of the lukewarm wine. The alcohol stung her torn lip. A heavy, bloody scent spread down her throat. Even so, the smell of disinfectant still tickled her nose, so she grabbed a handful of jelly from the drawer. She put all of the sugar-coated jelly, which were of different shapes and colors, into her mouth and chewed on them, and their sweet smell covered up the stench.

Her alarm sounded. She had to get ready for her lecture at the university. She cleaned up the desk and was about to click the browser window shut when an upbeat alarm rang through the room.

[Jelly Bean has sent you a message.]

You saw the responses on the message board, right? Do you even have the book, like you said? Come meet me with the book if you're not lying. If you can prove that you're telling the truth, I'll stop meddling with you and stay quiet on the site. Attached is a map with the location.

The lecture that day was a disaster. Hyeongyeong had replied to the message, saying that she would meet him there. She wasn't calm enough to give it rational thought.

What really got to her was the sense of deprivation. So she

wasn't the only one who had the book. There was someone else He had chosen. It was unthinkable. She couldn't even fall asleep that night. She felt anger rising deep within her—something she hadn't felt in a long time.

She stayed up all night in the dark room. She took out His book, whose pages she was so careful to even turn because she cherished it so, and began to peruse it. As she read over the contents of the book—which she had read so many times that she knew it by heart—she came to realize that she wasn't wrong. *I'm not wrong. Jelly Bean is the one who's got it wrong and should not be tolerated. Only one person can have His book. That's how it should be. I'm not wrong.* Hyeongyeong repeated these words over and over through the night.

The temperature hit a record high on the day they were supposed to meet. All set, Hyeongyeong headed to the appointed place. As she drove out of Seoul and onto an empty highway, a flashy billboard for New Seoul Park came into view. A dumb-looking bear was standing on one foot, carrying a huge arrow on its head. The lightbulbs on the arrow thoughtlessly flickered again and again.

As she neared her destination, Hyeongyeong pulled over to the side of the road. Then she looked herself over one last time. She didn't want to appear lacking in any way in front of Jelly Bean. In her mind, Jelly Bean was a professor from a wealthy family who just couldn't keep himself from flaunting his knowledge. She made an effort to stay composed. She was confident that she knew more about Him and the book than anyone else. The only reason why she had consented to seeing Jelly Bean in this complicated and inconvenient way was to see if he really had the book and if he could actually read it. If any of these two things turned out to be true, she had no intention of letting him get away with it. She fingered the item in her pocket.

To get to the location on the map he had sent, she had to take an unpaved road. After driving on the rugged road for a while, she arrived at a vacant lot between a mountain and a plot of land left unattended by the owners of the park. A human figure was standing alone in the middle of the lot.

Hyeongyeong calmly straightened her clothes before getting out of the car. The distance between the two closed with each step she took. As she saw Jelly Bean with her own eyes, a look of great dismay crossed her face. He had a small frame and was wearing a yellow-green park uniform so dirty that she was sure he hadn't washed it in a while; he had a bad posture, too, and was standing with his hands in his pockets. The disappointment she felt after seeing him in person was too staggering, and she was overcome by a sense of shame. Sensing her presence, Jelly Bean raised his head.

"Sodok?" he asked.

Hyeongyeong didn't bother to reply.

Slowly, she looked him up and down. His hair was unkempt, his eyes were sunken, and his mouth looked dirty. He seemed to be the epitome of a shut-in. He was nothing like what she had pictured repeatedly in her mind. He looked so pathetic that Hyeongyeong was at a loss for words.

She wanted to run back to her car immediately. But there was something she had to confirm. She stood there with her arms crossed, ready to hear what he had to say.

The New Seoul Park Jelly Massacre

"You have the book, don't you? Did you bring it?" he asked abruptly.

"Why should I tell you?" Hyeongyeong retorted.

"You don't sound so sure of yourself. Or were you lying after all, about having the book? I'm surprised, to be honest. I had no idea that you were a woman," Jelly Bean said, grinning.

Hyeongyeong shut her mouth tight. The comment wasn't worth responding to. Interpreting her silence in his favor, Jelly Bean came up to her, looking triumphant.

"You thought you were the only one who could read the book, didn't you? There isn't anyone in the world who has been chosen to be the one and only. The one who summons Him first, the one who brings about the Sabbath—that's who becomes the one and only. I will be the first—because the first is remembered forever. By Him, and by this world."

"I can't take any more of your crap," Hyeongyeong said, snorting. She had thought that he was full of himself, but the guy was nothing but a social outcast living in delusion. She felt genuinely offended. Of course she realized that not everyone on the site was as sincere in their faith as she was in hers, but the kind she detested above all were people like him. People like that didn't worship Him with all their heart. They were merely pretending to believe, hoping that one day, He would throw some crumbs at them.

Hyeongyeong uncrossed her arms to check her watch. Maybe a part of her wanted to rattle Jelly Bean by showing him something expensive, but honestly, she just didn't want to waste any more of her time. Based on what he had said so far, he was probably lying about having the book and being able to read it.

"I can't believe I wasted my time to come see a loser like you. So what is it you have to say?" Hyeongyeong asked, looking bored to death.

The look on her face must have triggered something in him. Jelly Bean's haggard face flushed red. Hyeongyeong went on, enjoying the way his face contorted, "Can you even read the book? The way I see it, you've never even turned a single page of the book. If you really do have it, what does it say on the first page?"

The corners of her lips curled up in a smile. There was no way he could answer that. She recited the answer in her mind: *We dance with the devil.*

Jelly Bean clenched his feeble hands into fists. His chest heaved up and down, and his expression had changed. It was so obvious what he was going to do next that Hyeongyeong was already bored. She regretted wasting her time and emotional energy on a loser like him. She was so ashamed of having been considered his equal, she couldn't bear it.

She was waiting for him to cross the line. It was like fishing with cheap bait. He took the bait much too quickly. With his eyes bloodshot from the repeated provocation, he suddenly lunged at her, uttering a strange sound—exactly as she had planned.

"Give me the book! I need the book to bring about the Sabbath!" he cried.

Hyeongyeong smiled faintly. She knew it; he had lied about having the book. So of course he couldn't have read it. He was worth nothing to her now, and she no longer had any use for him. The faces of her husband and mother-in-law, which she couldn't even properly recall now, overlapped with his. His face was nothing more than a stain—a huge stain she had to get rid of. With this thought in mind, she reached into her jacket pocket.

*

The omelet and rice dish, cold now, was sitting in front of her. Hyeongyeong stared at the omelet, which was so close that she could touch it if she just lowered her head and stuck her tongue out. Garnishing the yellow omelet was blue bleach. The fluorescent liquid gleamed in the darkness, spreading out in a zigzag line, as if it was ketchup that a child had gleefully squeezed out.

"Eat it," her mother-in-law said, shoving the plate in her face. Her eyes, surrounded by wrinkles, were full of menace. Hyeongyeong sat still with her mouth shut tight. Panju grabbed her chin with her hook-like hands and shook it violently. Screeching like a demon, she struggled with all her might to pry Hyeongyeong's mouth open.

"Eat it, eat it!" she screamed.

Hyeongyeong held out, clenching her teeth. She glared at Panju as coldly as she could. Her eyes stung as the blood rushed to them, but she had no intention of taking her eyes off the woman. Panju looked at her as though she were seeing an evil spirit. This time, her scrawny hands took hold of Hyeongyeong's hair and started yanking at it. It was mystifying how the old woman had such incredible power in her skinny little body. Hyeongyeong's hair, which had been tied neatly into a ponytail, came undone. The plate of omelet rice, sprinkled with bleach, fell to the floor and shattered with a crash. At the same time, Panju's hand, dry and withered like the bark of an old tree, slapped Hyeongyeong's face fiercely.

The sound of flesh hitting flesh echoed in the quiet living room. Without even touching her swollen cheek, Hyeongyeong kept her mouth shut and continued to glare at Panju. Panju gasped for breath, unable to control her skinny little body. Not a single thought came to Hyeongyeong's mind. She had no idea what to do, or even what she wanted to do, about this absurd but inevitable situation. Then out of the blue, the thought of the book came to her mind, along with the man's voice saying, "You'll be able to read it soon enough."

The raspy voice saying those baffling words hovered in her ears. Now, though, she felt that she understood.

That was her moment of salvation. The phone rang, piercing the intense silence. If this was a scene in a movie, the sound would have been a sign of misfortune to come. But Hyeongyeong was certain that it meant salvation, a helping hand extended by some unknown god. The sound would lead her to a new world.

"Hello," she said, picking up the phone.

She was right.

*

The sudden impact pushed Hyeongyeong to the hood of her car. She crashed into the car with a thud. She stared calmly at Jelly Bean, who had his hands around her neck. His eyes were out of focus. The whites of his eyes were pink now.

He became even more vicious as Hyeongyeong showed no

reaction. She could easily tell that the look on his glowering face was closer to that of fear than of rage—she had seen such a face before. Hyeongyeong opened her mouth in laughter. She found the guy, unable to even tighten his grip on her thin neck, quite hilarious. His face was just like Panju's that day. She had been saved by Him that day, but this time, she had to find a way out herself.

By now she was starting to wonder if it was His will through which she had met Jelly Bean. There were no meaningless coincidences in the world. Hyeongyeong pulled out from her pocket the item she had brought and stretched out her arm. Then with all her might, she plunged the syringe—filled with an anesthetic drug for animals—deep into his arm.

*

The sudden phone call informed Hyeongyeong of her husband's death. The cause of death was a car accident from drunk driving. Panju's hand shook terribly as she took the receiver from her. Hyeongyeong's heart began to beat to a strange rhythm, as if it was a sign foreshadowing something. Panju put the receiver down without a word. The raging feelings had vanished into thin air; her eyes, like empty glass beads, fell on Hyeongyeong. Hyeongyeong no longer cared if the feeling in those eyes was that of anger, emptiness, or sorrow.

"It's your fault," Panju spat out, staring at Hyeongyeong. Her voice sounded hollow. Panju turned around, hastily put on a coat, and headed to the front door. Her face was so green it was as if she had stage makeup on. Hyeongyeong took in the scene as if she was watching a boring comedy movie. Then came the ludicrous climax: Panju, rushing toward the shoe cabinet, reeled dramatically.

Panju fell back with a thud, her body stiff like a mannequin. Her small, light head fell on the ornamental rock that her son had so treasured, hitting it with a delightful thump. It sounded like a fist punching a hole in a paper screen or the boom of a drum at the start of marching music. To Hyeongyeong, it felt like a signal.

Panju's head bounced off the floor once, then settled, again with a delightful thud. A pool of dark red blood began to spread out from the caved-in head. Her eyes, wide open, were fixed on Hyeongyeong, or perhaps on the family portrait behind her. Hyeongyeong stood still in the darkness until the blood began to wet her toes. She stared at the mop, which Panju had slipped on, and the spray bottle of bleach next to it. Her brain cells, which had always felt like they were steeped in disinfectant, began to awaken one by one.

A sweet, fragrant smell was coming from somewhere. It was so overpowering that Hyeongyeong felt as if her brain would melt. She looked around to see where it was coming from. It turned out that the sweet, pleasant smell was wafting out from her own bag. As she rummaged through her bag, her hand came upon the book with the old leather cover.

She pulled the book out and opened it to a random page. The book gleamed peculiarly in the dark apartment. She blinked her eyes. The strange characters that had looked more like drawings before came alive and began to wriggle around. Then they came to a stop, having taken on different shapes.

The New Seoul Park Jelly Massacre

Hyeongyeong stared intently at the pages. She could read the words. Words professing certain truths about the world came spilling into her mind. At the same time, she recalled the voice of the man who had spoken to her. She knew instinctively that he had helped her. And she knew: she had been born again. And she had been chosen.

*

Jelly Bean's rake-like hands fell from her neck. Hyeongyeong caught her breath as he screamed. Her flushed face gradually returned to normal. Jelly Bean pulled out the syringe from his arm and shouted, his eyes full of fear as he stared at her, "What is this? What did you do?"

It was priceless how frightened he was, screaming in fear. Leaning against her car and gasping for breath, Hyeongyeong looked him over. It would be a little while before the anesthetic took effect.

"Stop it, both of you! Are you crazy?" cried out an unfamiliar voice from the building behind her. Hyeongyeong frowned. The guy, who looked like Jelly Bean's co-worker, didn't seem to have the guts to step forward and intervene. At his appearance, Jelly Bean seemed to remember something and shouted, "You got it all on video, right?"

The guy nodded, looking bewildered. At that moment, Jelly Bean staggered dramatically. Hyeongyeong began a countdown in her mind. All he had left now was his bravado. Pointing to his co-worker with a finger—not in an especially threatening way—he said in a trembling voice, "I-I got you on video. I'm going to post it on the web. Everything about you—your personal life, the fact that you're a devil worshiper, everything. I've got nothing to lose, but that's not the case with you, is it?"

Then he began to run toward his co-worker, his hands stretched out. A wave of irritation washed over Hyeongyeong. She just wanted to put an end to this pathetic nonsense. She took a look around. The gray steel reinforcement bars around her formed a strange harmony with the colorful ride parts. Soon her eyes fell on something just right. She walked over to the dusty Dream Teddy bumper car.

What she picked up was a red-and-white candy cane. Though it was in the shape of a candy cane, it was made of iron and quite heavy. She liked the weighty feel of the iron bar in her hand. She went after Jelly Bean, dragging the candy cane behind her on the ground. The sound of metal scraping cement grated on her ears.

Jelly Bean's movements became noticeably slow—the anesthetic must have started to take effect. Hyeongyeong began to walk faster. She looked straight ahead, her mouth firmly shut. She looked at nothing but what was in front of her. As she chased after Jelly Bean, her eyes met those of his frightened co-worker. Hyeongyeong took a deep breath and raised the hand holding the candy cane high up in the air. Jelly Bean called out to his co-worker with a stiffened tongue. It kept him from pronouncing his name properly.

"S-Sajun," he uttered.

Thwack! She hit him, and the sensation of striking something solid shook up her arm. Jelly Bean collapsed as helplessly as a scarecrow without its pole. Again, Hyeongyeong raised the candy cane. She struck him on the head—once, twice, three times—as though hitting a golf ball with a club. Hot blood splattered onto her face. It wasn't pleasant, but it didn't feel so bad either.

Jelly Bean stopped moving. Looking at his caved-in head, Hyeongyeong recalled the moment when her mother-in-law died. She grinned and flung down the candy cane. Drops of blood trickled down the curve of the cane. She wiped at her bloody face, but the blood had already dried and didn't come off easily.

Something fell with a flop. She looked over to where the sound had come from. The guy—Jelly-Bean's co-worker—had collapsed on the ground. His cell phone was by his feet. So Jelly Bean had done some thinking with his puny little brain. She wondered for a second if she should call him daring or cowardly. But she realized that there was no reason for her to care—after all, he no longer existed.

So the guy's name was Sajun. She looked at him sitting on the ground, trembling like a leaf. He was better off than Jelly Bean but didn't look all that different from him. Hyeongyeong's eyes were fixed on Sajun's pocket. A wad of crumpled-up fifty-thousand won bills was sticking out from the pocket. She went up to him and picked up the phone from the ground.

A message came on the screen informing that the video had been saved. She pressed YES when she was asked if she wanted to see the video. The video, a little over ten minutes, began to play; it ended at the part where she raised the cane. There was almost nothing she could see clearly as the beginning of the video was very shaky and out of focus, but she had better make sure. Hyeongyeong composed herself. She put on her usual responsible face and extended him an offer: "I like your video. I'll buy it from you."

She handed him a business card. With his knees on the

ground, Sajun took it with both hands. The lustrous white paper had Hyeongyeong's bloodied fingerprints on it. A look of both fear and hope crossed his eyes as he looked up at Hyeongyeong. She smiled. She knew that he wouldn't be able to resist her offer.

The whole time he was digging the ground, Sajun kept mumbling some mysterious numbers. He looked fine on the outside, but he seemed to be as nuts as the other guy. Hyeongyeong had made an excellent choice. It would be safer to bait him into being an accomplice than to threaten and terrify him. He had taken the bait so eagerly that it made her laugh.

While Sajun was digging a hole for the body, Hyeongyeong did some research on Jelly Bean. She took a picture of the ID card she had taken out of his wallet and sent it to the private detective she had previously been in contact with. The reply came promptly. She checked the material, which summarized his basic personal information and background.

Having read through the material, she burst out laughing. Jelly Bean had no one around him—no family, no friends. She couldn't help thinking that He was helping her. There was no one to even report him missing. Jelly Bean had been completely isolated from the world. This was simply too easy. "This is a good sign," she mumbled to herself. She sensed something great on the horizon. She felt like she was on cloud nine.

After rolling Jelly Bean's body into the hole, she threw in the candy cane weapon as well. Sajun covered the contorted body with dirt, still mumbling those numbers of his. Hyeongyeong turned on the ignition of her car. The sky was orange. The sun was beginning to set behind the mountain.

The New Seoul Park Jelly Massacre

The two of them, having taken care of the body, got in the car and drove down the mountain. They could smell something sweet—something very, very sweet. Hyeongyeong hadn't smelled anything so sweet since she had been at that apartment. She felt as if He were praising her. Whether this smell was an illusion or reality didn't matter. She mumbled in satisfaction: "I knew it—He is on my side."

When they arrived at the lot, she handed Sajun the money she had brought. It wasn't even a box full of money, just an envelope. But he took it, his face radiating with joy, as if he had found salvation or something. She was suddenly filled with a curious sense of kinship. It had occurred to her that the way he was looking at the money was probably similar to the way she looked when she was thinking of Him. Though they had different objects of worship, they both worshiped something or someone. At that moment, she felt as though she was Sajun's god. Savoring the feeling of elation that came over her, as well as the subtle sense of immorality that came from seeing herself as His equal, she said benevolently: "Call me if you need more."

Sajun nodded, then ran off. He looked so pathetic and small as he disappeared into the distance. Hyeongyeong got back into her car. Even after she had gotten off the side road of the lot, the sweet smell continued to pervade the air. She drove on, giving herself over to the dreamy scent. The road ahead seemed interminable. No matter how long she drove, there was no end in sight.

A sign read 1 KM TO NEW SEOUL PARK—a sign she had passed several times already. The road seemed to be alive and moving, like an enormous organism in the form of a coffin. The sweet smell grew stronger by the minute. She knew she had taken the road that led away from the park, but somehow, ahead of her now was the glittering signboard of New Seoul Park. The sky was a peculiar purple color, as the dark blue of the night mingled with the red sky. It looked pink in a way. Dazed, Hyeongyeong stared at the theme park spread out before her like a mirage. Jelly Bean's words flashed through her mind: *"The Sabbath is coming to New Seoul Park. He is coming."*

"Oh!" she exclaimed, almost like a death cry. She had come to a powerful realization. How could she not have been aware of the obvious meaning behind this mysterious phenomenon? She got out of the car. The road had led her to New Seoul Park. The sweet smell was coming from Him. Hyeongyeong knew intuitively that He was calling to her.

Her heart began to beat rapidly. She had to answer His call. She, as a priest and intercessor, had offered the arrogant Jelly Bean as a sacrifice for the Sabbath. Everything was happening according to His will. The Sabbath was here.

Hyeongyeong approached the entrance of the park. Her slow steps quickened with every second that passed. The closer she got to the inside of the park, the louder the screams that rang like music in her ears grew. *This is a festival—a festival to welcome Him,* she thought. She had to hold herself back from bursting into song and laughter.

At the entrance were nothing but pools of jelly—no one and nothing alive. She walked over the sticky pools of jelly and into the park. As she crossed the boundary, she felt something she had experienced before—the sensation of throwing herself into pudding. A very warm and moist air enveloped her. She looked at the scene spread out before her, a theme park full of sweet jelly. The people there were posing no threat to one another and were simply all melting into soft jelly. The song-like screams that had rung through the park soon died away.

Silence fell over New Seoul Park. The only sound was that of jelly falling in globs. Hyeongyeong couldn't tell how much time had passed. She sensed a shadow beckoning her. She tried to focus her eyes on the shadow. Someone was standing in front of the carousel that was still going around. He was the only one who had a form of any kind amid all the shapeless jelly. Hyeongyeong knew instinctively that it was Him.

Filled with emotion, she approached Him. The figure before her eyes looked like a man over forty, but also like a woman in her twenties; then again, it looked like a very young child. Its ambiguous, shadowy form stood in front of Hyeongyeong. One thing was sure, though: it had a powerful presence. Hyeongyeong said, her voice trembling, "You've really come."

She smiled in ecstasy. The figure reached out a hand with an ambiguous expression on its face—it was neither smiling nor crying. She couldn't tell what He looked like at all. He was right there in front of her, and yet she could not see him. She followed His movements with her eyes. She knelt down and He smiled. It was a very benevolent smile.

She looked at the pink gem-like jelly falling from his fingertips. He hadn't said a word, but she was able to understand His intentions immediately. "That's salvation," she mumbled. She caught the falling salvation in her hands. Now she could be with Him as a participant of the Sabbath. She felt that she had become His servant at last. She felt full of faith. She put all the jelly in her hands into her mouth. The pink lump—sweeter than anything she had ever tasted or any moment she had ever experienced—melted in her mouth.

Overwhelmed, Hyeongyeong closed her eyes. When she opened them again, He had long gone. But she wasn't sad, even though she couldn't see Him anymore—she knew that He would always be with her. Her body was growing heavier. It was an extraordinary sensation. Her skin, her muscles, her bones—things that had functioned systematically and had been solid—were turning soft. It wasn't painful. In contrast to her body, which was now giving in to gravity, her mind was becoming very light—so light that she felt like she could fly. She wondered about the end of the Sabbath, which she would reach through His guidance after leaving her heavy, weary body. She closed her eyes and gave herself over to the sensation of falling into a massive pudding.

The puddle in front of the carousel was exceptionally round—it was a perfect, precise circle. The men in blue uniforms took a long look at the puddle. A very fine suit was tangled in the sticky jelly. One of the men pulled down a mask that covered half his face and said, "You know what? I haven't seen the director lately."

The words "Gwangnan Cleaning" were clearly printed on their uniforms. Another man replied as he picked up some things with long tongs, "I know. She used to always come on time."

"Nothing's happened to her, right? I mean, there's been some weird stuff going on lately."

"What could've happened to her? It's obvious. She's just changed."

The New Seoul Park Jelly Massacre

"But she isn't like that."

"You never know."

The man who had first brought up the subject dragged over a huge vacuum cleaner and turned on the power. The vacuum cleaner loudly sucked up the pink puddle. The men, who had been talking about trivial things, took a bottle of blue bleach from a cart and poured the liquid on the ground. The spot where Hyeongyeong had melted away soon turned blue. After some vigorous mopping, nothing at all remained.

Friends without Names

0

"More than five-hundred in my bank account, plus twenty from that part-time job, minus forty for food, nine for phone, and thirty for living expenses … How did I spend so much? And minus twenty for the monthly rent … Damn, and then there's tax," Sajun mumbled anxiously. No matter how many calculations he did, nothing had changed compared to before. The sum that had seemed frighteningly large when he had taken the envelope from Yu didn't seem so big anymore. But it wasn't like he had splurged or anything.

The biggest problem, of course, was the monthly rent. He had been forced to leave the dormitory and find an apartment when the park shut down. But housing prices in Seoul were exorbitant. The money from Yu was nowhere near enough for leasing a room on a deposit basis. So he rented a gosiwon room, which didn't require a big deposit, and as he paid off his little debts and bought what he needed, the money quickly dwindled. He spent all day on the web searching for a new job but was struggling to come across anything suitable. He felt like he was at a dead end.

As he refreshed the browser, he noticed a job post. It was for Gwangnan Cleaning.

WE ARE HIRING
: No Job Experience Required
: Simple Cleaning Job
: Room & Board Provided; Overtime Pay & Holiday Pay; Weekly Salary
: Strong, Hardworking People Wanted

Sajun recalled a newspaper article he happened to see a while ago. It had said that Gwangnan Cleaning was taking on the cleaning of New Seoul Park.

The bizarre case of the disappearances at New Seoul Park was all over the media for a while. Countless people had disappeared, leaving nothing but sweet jelly in their place. It had all happened in less than two hours. Experts had been brought in from abroad to investigate the case, but not a single clue had been found.

As time passed, people wanted to put the incident behind them rather than find out what had really taken place. It was fear of the unknown—it wasn't easy to accept the fact that something inexplicable had happened in the world you lived in. When things had calmed down a bit, New Seoul Park seized the opportunity to sign a contract with Gwangnan Cleaning. That extensive plot of land couldn't be left unused for long.

Sajun searched online for the picture from the article. Yu Hyeongyeong, the director of the company, wasn't in the picture, even though the contract was an important event.

"Call me if you need more," she had said, handing him the envelope. The more he dwelled on those words, the harder time he had shaking off the thought that he should have asked for more in the first place. It wasn't right that he had to bury Yeongdu's dead body for an amount that fit in a single envelope.

He took out the business card Yu had given him. His call did go through but no one picked up. She must be avoiding him on purpose. He could have gotten at least twice as much from her with the video he had. He had to somehow find a way to see her again. He took a closer look at the job post. The pay was much higher than average, and to top it off, room and board was provided. Sajun did a quick calculation.

"With room and board taken care of, I wouldn't have to spend any more of my money. And with the basic pay of three hundred a month, plus overtime pay for working three nights a week … Oh, and it says there's an incentive, so I could probably add an extra fifty to that. If I saved all that, the total would come to …"

He came to the conclusion that no matter how he looked at it, applying for the job was the best thing to do. It would be better to save money on rent, even if it was just for a few months, than wasting time in this tiny little room. Besides, Yu was famous for working side by side with her employees. He would have a chance of seeing her again while on the job.

Sajun recalled the grotesque scene that he had seen that day at the theme park, but he still clicked the "Apply" button without hesitation. It was only jelly after all, and what had happened that night was so unreal that he could just think of it as a dream. Dreams fade away once you're awake. What's truly terrifying is the reality that comes after a dream. Sajun submitted the application in a hurry.

1

Jelly's first memory was of the rough feel of cement. She sensed someone's foot stepping on her and was slowly awakened to an odd, squishy sound. She raised herself up.

"Ow, my head!" she cried out automatically.

The pawprint on her head was comically clear. It didn't hurt, but it was something she had never experienced before. Jelly stared straight ahead with her round eyes. The pawprint belonged to a cat passing by. The cat, who had walked off into the distance after stepping on her, came to a stop and looked back at her. Jelly waved her arm in greeting, and the cat came toward her. New pawprints appeared in the opposite direction from the ones on the ground. With her yellow eyes sparkling, the cat said, "So you're alive."

"Alive?" Jelly asked.

The cat pointed down. Clinging to the ground were others like Jelly.

"They don't move or talk. I've been walking around, leaving countless pawprints, but you're the only one who's said anything to me."

Jelly blinked her eyes. She reached out a hand, with which she had been rubbing her head, and stared at her transparent surface. They were all of the same color and texture, so why couldn't the others move or talk? She couldn't understand. She asked, "What do I look like?"

The cat stared at her for a moment and then said, "Come with me."

Jelly moved her round body. She didn't have legs that looked like pillars, like the cat did, but when she tried to move the lower part of her body, the part touching the ground began to wriggle. Her body was definitely moving forward.

The cat led the way. Jelly moved as fast as she could so as not to fall behind. The middle of her body thumped the ground. She moved forward, looking busily around. The cat stopped now and then, waiting for Jelly, who was much slower than she was.

The two finally arrived at an old castle with a sign that said MIRRORLAND. This place, too, was full of jelly that didn't move. The two headed inside, where they found a room with mirrors on all the walls. The cat pointed to one of the mirrors and said, "This is what you look like."

Jelly took in her reflection for the very first time. Her body was round like a waterdrop, with two eyes that were round as well. The pawprint on her head was fading away, so the top of her head was becoming smooth again. The countless mirrors in this maze-like space reflected the two of them. Jelly asked the cat in the mirror: "Have you seen another jelly who moves like me?"

The cat slowly shook her head.

Jelly left Mirrorland. She descended from the castle entrance and touched the mounds of jelly sprawled out on the ground with her swollen hands, but they didn't budge. She tried poking at them, leaving marks on them like the cat had. Still, they didn't show any reaction. She felt cold and empty, as though there was a big hole in the middle of her body. At that moment she heard the cat say, "Don't worry. I'm alone, too."

The cat jumped down from the castle stairs and stood next to Jelly. Her eyes shining, Jelly asked, "Are you really alone, too?"

"I am," the cat said, raising a paw and leaving another mark on Jelly's head. Jelly patted the clear pawprint. For some reason, she liked how the pawprint made the surface bumpy. The chill that had made her feel cold and empty gradually dissipated.

Jelly followed the cat around all day. The cat seemed annoyed.

"Stop following me. Do you know how annoying it is when something sticky clings to you?"

But whenever Jelly was in danger—when she lost her way or fell into a chink in a ride—the cat appeared out of nowhere and extended a helping paw. Jelly liked the cat. The cat was brusque but kind, and she was always near her even when she was out of view. Whenever she thought of the cat, Jelly felt as though there were bubbles rising inside of her. The days went by in peace.

It was the perfect day to lie around in the square. Then a strange noise was heard. The cat rushed to her feet and dragged Jelly under the bench. The things that came out of the swiftly moving machine were organisms Jelly had never seen before. The cat called them "humans."

"Quick, we need to hide," the cat said.

Jelly didn't understand why they had to hide, but she decided to do as the cat instructed for the time being. She hid under the bench with the cat and observed the humans. They were exchanging words she couldn't understand very well and went around as though the park belonged to them.

The New Seoul Park Jelly Massacre

"Don't ever let them see you," the yellow-eyed cat cautioned, looking Jelly in the face. Humans returned to the park again and again. Later, they even set up huge boxes and began to live inside them, bringing others to live with them. They began to occupy more and more of the land, and as a result, Jelly and the cat had less and less space to play in. Something began to rise in Jelly—not soft little bubbles but big, seething bubbles.

"It's not fair. This used to be our playground," Jelly said.

"Things like this happen all the time," the cat said, looking indifferent. Her face seemed to say that this was as expected as the sun rising in the east. She looked calm and composed, as well as sick and tired of it all.

Then shortly after, the monsters appeared. Jelly understood at last why the cat had cautioned her. The monsters—which they called "vacuum cleaners"—sucked up all the jellies in the park, making frightening noises as they went around with the humans. Once eaten, the jellies never returned. Jelly tried to keep herself from screaming whenever she saw the black mouths of the vacuum cleaners.

The jellies in the park quickly began to disappear. Jelly could no longer spend much time outside. She stayed in the café—her hideout—during most of the day. The only times she could go outside were late at night or early in the morning when the vacuum cleaners weren't in action. Whenever she heard the whir of the vacuum cleaners, she curled up inside a cabinet drawer in the café and covered her ears. Each time, the cat said dryly, "It's all right. It's all going to end one day."

And amazingly, the words calmed her every time.

Jelly thought about those words often. They were like a magic spell. On days when she was sad, or when she almost got caught by humans, or when the vacuum cleaners were unusually loud, she could endure by thinking of those words. It was all going to end one day. All the bad and hard things would pass in the end—all the good things, too, of course. Then a question came to her mind. How did the cat know this wonderful and sad truth? Shaking the cat, who was getting ready for a nap, she asked, "Were you always alone before you met me?"

The cat pondered for a long time before answering, "Not always, but they all left."

"How come?"

"They had no choice. I've lived for a very long time—I'm older than this theme park."

The theme park was very big. It would have taken a very long time to build such a huge park. Jelly couldn't even imagine how long the cat must have lived. She imagined that the cat must have been very lonely, walking around such a big place all by herself. She must have had friends who were with her for a time. But she had no one left now. Jelly didn't want to leave her. She didn't want to leave the cat all alone.

"I'm not going to leave you," Jelly said.

The cat yawned in reply. Jelly couldn't understand for the life of her what the cat's age had to do with friends, but she was sure that she wouldn't be like those friends. She couldn't picture herself without the cat. As she got used to the whir of the vacuum cleaner echoing through her mind, Jelly slipped into a dream.

2

The first time she heard Jelly's voice, the cat couldn't believe her ears. She had turned around and seen something that looked like a big drop of water waving its hand. She had never seen such a creature in her life. Jelly that talked and moved—it wasn't jelly, and it certainly wasn't human.

After checking herself in Mirrorland, Jelly had looked confused.

"Don't worry. I'm alone, too," the cat had impulsively said to the crestfallen Jelly. When she thought about it later on, she couldn't understand why she had said such a thing; then with Jelly clinging to her all the time, she felt so flustered that she forgot all about it. Jelly was persistent. The cat would make a show of climbing a tree, trying to aggravate Jelly, or she would roll Jelly away like a ball whenever she made the effort to come close. Even so, Jelly followed her everywhere. The cat often thought of the old woman's daughter when she was with Jelly. They were very much alike in that they did something to annoy her whenever they had a chance.

"I'm not going to leave you."

They even said the same meaningless words. Jelly's round eyes had shone with resolution as she said those words. The cat had let out a long yawn. She wasn't going to leave. Sure. The cat didn't believe her. She knew, of course, that Jelly wasn't lying. Jelly was just too young to know that leaving or not leaving wasn't up to you. In this world, nothing lasted forever.

Afterwards, Jelly kept saying the words over and over again, as if by habit. Words have power to them. That power has a big impact on the soft, spineless lump called the heart. It confuses the heart and makes it infinitely vulnerable. Unaware of that, Jelly made empty promises she couldn't keep—that she wouldn't leave, that she would stay forever with the cat. Before she knew it, the cat found herself being swayed by those enchanting words. She really hadn't wanted things to turn out this way. Jelly, who didn't know anything, smiled in innocence as she rolled around on a sofa in the café.

The whir of the vacuum cleaners could be heard every day. The mounds of jelly that had been all over the park continued to disappear. Watching the bored faces of the humans, the cat wondered if they knew that those lumps of jelly had once been human like them. Did they know but just didn't care, or had they just accepted the fact, having no other choice? Humans were always cleaning up something that was there and building something new in its place. Jelly trembled in fear when she saw the vacuum cleaners, but the cat knew that one day, everything would pass.

Then one day, the cat saw a familiar face among the people in blue clothes who came during the day. It was the human who had been inside the furry creature that used to dance in front of the carousel.

<u>3</u>

Sajun took a bus to New Seoul Park and found that it didn't look that different from the last time he had seen it. The only difference was that the sticky, pink slime was more or less dry now. It would take a ton of work to get rid of it all. On the first day of work he was assigned a room and given necessary articles, as well as a brief orientation about the job. The whole time his attention was focused on where Yu could be, but he couldn't find any trace of her.

During the first few days on the job, Sajun tried to find out what was going on. There was no sign of Yu anywhere. As the staff began to talk about how the director had changed and no longer bothered to come work with them anymore, Sajun made a secret trip to the vacant lot. First, he had to find out whether Yu was alive or dead. Her car wasn't in the lot. After combing through the area, he finally found her car in the parking lot at the entrance of the park. The fact that the car was there meant that she hadn't made it back home.

After checking to make sure that there was no one around, Sajun broke the car window. He took a quick look inside but didn't see anything worth much. There was a purse in the corner but there was no cash in it. He put the cards back in the purse to avoid any suspicion later on.

"But what about the money? Is there no way of getting more now?" he mumbled. Then something crossed his mind, his cell phone, which Yu had taken. It still had the video of Yeongdu's murder on it. If Yu had disappeared, there was a good chance that his phone would be here somewhere. If he cropped the video a bit, just the beginning and the end, and sold a muted version to reporters, he could probably make good money on it. A big smile appeared on his face. He rushed back to Yu's car. He ransacked the car, but his phone was nowhere to be seen.

"Damn, where did she put it?"

If it wasn't in the car, maybe it was in the park. He would have to look carefully starting tomorrow, while he was cleaning. The mounds of jelly covering the theme park had all kinds of daily necessities and cell phones in them. As a rule, the things that were found while cleaning had to be stored separately before being sent for investigation, but some of the workers took things that were in decent condition and sold them secondhand.

"I really hope no one's sold it already," he mumbled.

He would be in great trouble if someone had. His face wasn't in the video, but the phone was in his name. He broke into a cold sweat. He did a quick search on his new phone. He looked up "how to track a lost phone," and after learning how to find the location through the phone account, he checked the map with trembling hands. There was a red dot on it. The dot was pointing to the last tracked location of the phone—a spot near the carousel. The carousel was close to the container where he was staying. The phone hadn't been turned on since that day, which meant that no third party had touched it. Relief flooded through him. If he thoroughly searched the storage room as well as the area around the carousel, he would be able to find it for sure. He had to find it. He walked, repeating the same words over and over again as if chanting a spell.

It was almost midnight already. Sajun couldn't see anything in the darkness as there was no electricity anywhere other than in the square, where the containers were. He heard a cat meowing somewhere, which spooked him. Just then, something lumpy flashed before his eyes. He screamed, staggering backwards. Something soft touched his ankle. He fell with a piercing cry. He managed to pull out his phone and turned on its flashlight. He shone it in front of him. A cat with glittering eyes was sitting there, its paws neatly together.

The New Seoul Park Jelly Massacre

"Oh, damn …"

Sajun got up and shook the dust off. The cat hissed and disappeared into a thicket. Feeling disturbed, Sajun returned to his container and carefully made his way over to the cabinet in the corner. Everyone was fast asleep, exhausted from the day's work. The cabinet door creaked as he opened it but no one woke up. He carefully looked through the chief's uniform pocket and pulled out the key to the storage room.

4

The first thing she heard was the frightening sound of a vacuum cleaner. Hiding in the cabinet drawer, she closed her eyes tight. A familiar yet alien scene unfolded in the darkness. She was lying on a sofa in a sunny room. A woman was vacuuming the floor. The vacuum cleaner and the woman didn't seem frightening at all. Was it because it was a dream? Though she looked tired, the woman had a gentle smile on her face, and the vacuum cleaner was much smaller than the monsters going around the park.

"… Time to wake up," the woman said, coming toward her.

That was the last thing Jelly heard before she opened her eyes. She felt sad for some reason. She couldn't remember what the woman had called her, no matter how hard she tried.

She had more dreams after that. She was reminded of them when she saw the snacks the cat had gotten from humans, the things in the café, the scenery outside the window, and even the faces of strangers. She had never thought about memories before she had these dreams. But lately, she had been wondering how she had known that a cat was called a cat and that she was called Jelly as soon as she had opened her eyes and entered this world.

"There might be more to me than I know," she said to herself.

Feeling excited, she tried to recall her dreams. In the images that came to her mind, the theme park was noisy and fun. The park was mostly full of people, but they didn't go around with vacuum cleaners in their hands or threatening looks on their faces. She would have spent all day looking at the scene if she could.

The dreams always ended at an obscure point. Jelly would wake up to silence, with even the cat asleep. In those moments, a strange forlorn feeling washed over her. She felt as though she had been kicked out of a festival she had been enjoying. Her body grew increasingly heavier.

It was so early in the morning that the sun wasn't even up yet. Thinking back on her dream and about the damp night air, she lay there, her heavy body slouching. She looked more like a sliding pile of mud than a round drop of water. She must have touched the sleeping cat's paw as she stirred about because the cat opened her eyes. Still lying down, Jelly asked, "Cat, you were right next to me when I woke up. Is there anything you know about me?"

"How am I supposed to know something about you that you don't even know?"

The reply was expected, but still feeling dejected, Jelly curled up into a ball.

Late at night, when the humans were all inside their boxes sleeping, Jelly took walks in the park with the cat. It was the only time they could walk around freely. As they went around, they saw many strange and marvelous things and even things which Jelly had seen in her dreams, such as wallets, rings, and straws. She would pick up the things she liked and stick them to her head.

She was lucky that night. She found something called a cell phone under a horse on the carousel. Jelly picked up the thing, which she had seen many times in her dreams, with her short arm. The flat, rectangular object was quite heavy.

"I've seen this before. Humans love it," she said.

"That's right. They can't live without it," the cat said in agreement.

There were so many shops selling cell phones on the street she had walked down in her dreams. She had pestered the woman for a long time for that rectangular thing. Whenever she did so, an odd look appeared on the woman's face—Jelly couldn't tell if she was crying or smiling. That face remained vivid in her mind. Jelly took a good, long look at the cell phone she had picked up.

The phone showed nothing but a black screen—it didn't seem to do anything else. Jelly had seen humans talking on it and listening to music with it, but she wasn't sure how. Maybe it was broken. After fumbling with it for a while, she stuck it firmly to the side of her head. The phone clung to her with ease.

"Humans always talk with this thing stuck to the side of their face," she said.

The cat laughed quietly. Jelly, happy with the unexpected find, hummed as she walked. The cat followed behind, as though to escort her. The lights were all off, and the path was pitch dark. Only the two eyes of the cat gleamed white in the darkness. Suddenly the cat came to a stop. Jelly turned around and looked in front of her. A human in a blue uniform was walking toward them. No human should be out at this hour. Jelly's body stiffened in shock. The cat looked back at her and shouted.

5

"Hurry, run to the fence!"

The human who was approaching from a distance looked familiar. He was the one who had been inside the furry creature. The cat recalled how he had spat out curses. She had to hide Jelly somewhere. There was no way a human would leave an alive and moving jelly alone. The cat shoved Jelly behind herself and stepped forward. But something caught her tail, pulling it taut. It was Jelly. In a tearful voice she said, "No! What if the vacuum monster sucks you up, too!"

"They don't eat cats."

"I don't want you to go away."

As Jelly clung to the cat, the human drew near. It really wasn't easy going around with Jelly. Without warning, the cat rolled her over to the side. Jelly made it into the thicket just before the human stepped on her. Quickly, the cat touched the human's foot. The human, who fell with a shriek, shone his flashlight on her. The cat meowed to try and get his attention.

After the human left, the cat found Jelly hiding in the thicket. She was curled up into a ball with her eyes closed. The cat stroked her, saying, "The human is gone."

Jelly burrowed herself into the cat's arms. The cat could feel her soft, trembling surface. It was cold and wet, but she liked the way it felt. The cat raised a paw and drew her close.

"You little scaredy-cat," the cat said, half scolding and half comforting as she licked Jelly's round surface. It had a sweet, fruity flavor to it. Still clinging to the other side of Jelly was the cell phone. Narrowing her eyes, the cat pointed to the phone and asked, "Aren't you going to take that thing off?"

"No, I'm going to keep it on," Jelly said, still hugging the cat. The cat meowed quietly in reply. Even afterwards, Jelly kept the cell phone on her head. She would often tilt her head to one side, imitating the way humans talked into phones. The cat found it funny and cute, and didn't say anything about it.

But the cat wondered: How had Jelly known how to use the phone? The humans in blue clothes didn't use their phones much during the day. The cat had seen them use their phones at night around their boxes, but Jelly had never gone near there because she was too afraid. The cat felt as though she had a fish bone stuck in her throat.

6

It was past two in the morning. Sajun came sneaking out of his container and headed to the storage room. He had scoured the area near the carousel during the day but hadn't found anything. The storage room was his last hope. Feeling anxious, he went into the dark room. Inside, there were piles of objects covered in jelly.

Electronic devices, such as cell phones, were kept in the farthest corner. Sajun walked toward a metal shelf that looked as though it was about to collapse and shone his flashlight on it. The phones, jumbled up in a pile in a plastic basket, still had sticky jelly clinging to them.

"Please let me find you here," Sajun said as he put on the gloves he had brought and began to rummage through the pile. The remaining jelly stuck to his hands. He busily turned the phones' power on and off. A few of them were the same model, but none of them were actually his. In the end, he had to turn around empty handed. He quietly locked the door, and an overwhelming sense of anxiety came over him.

It was uncanny. The phone wasn't in the theme park or in the storage room, and it had never been turned back on—it seemed to have vanished into thin air. It wasn't like the phone had feet and could run.

The moon was unusually bright. On his way back to his container, he was surprised to come across a pair of yellow eyes. A cat with black and white fur was staring at him with those bright yellow eyes. He realized that the cat looked familiar. It was Dream Kitty, the cat who had sat by the bench, munching on the snacks people gave her while he danced in front of the carousel. Then, too, the cat had looked at him with those same yellow eyes as though she pitied him.

"Damn cat!"

Sajun slowly approached the cat. Dream Kitty didn't make a sound; she just stood there, her eyes gleaming, before disappearing into the thicket. Sajun stared dejectedly into the darkness that had swallowed the cat. A strange thought occurred to him.

The cat showed up whenever Sajun was looking for his phone. She would stare at him for a long time with those creepy yellow eyes before disappearing. It was as though she was mocking him. The cat always seemed to look down on him. Maybe even now, she was hiding somewhere in the darkness, watching him. He wondered if the cat was the reason why he couldn't find his phone. The thought was so absurd that he couldn't even voice it out loud. But the suspicion, now that it had been planted, kept growing.

He returned to his container, his eyes bloodshot. He put the storage room key back in its place and lay down on his bed, but he had trouble falling asleep. The cat's yellow eyes seemed to be gleaming at him in the darkness.

7

Jelly was lying stretched out on the pavement where she had first met the cat, blinking her eyes. There were stars sparsely scattered throughout the sky. She reached out her short arm but couldn't touch any of the stars. She felt lonely. Why did she feel this way when she had the cat?

After lying there for a while, Jelly began to move toward the bench. In the past, she hadn't been able to do anything without the cat. She hadn't even been able to climb up onto the bench and had to have the cat prop her up, but now she could use her sticky surface to climb up the bench leg. The bench leg was cold. She had a dream a couple of nights ago about sitting on a bench like this, waiting and waiting for someone. Her buttocks had been warm at the time because it was midday, but now it was the opposite. Jelly sat still and looked around.

She saw something sparkling in the flowerbed near the bench. She felt drawn to it somehow and approached it as if by an unseen force. It was a purple hairpin in the shape of a conch. It felt familiar to her and made her feel nostalgic. She picked it up and turned it this way and that under the moonlight. It gave off different colors depending on the angle. Jelly knew that she had seen it before.

She saw someone's dry and wavy hair, with the pin adorning it, swaying before her eyes. Jelly recalled the gentle, kind hands that had put the pin in her hair. She saw the hem of a dress as someone came running to her from a distance. That person was calling out a name. It was her name.

"Jua!"

Her mom, wearing a blue dress, was running toward her. Her eyes were red, and her face was contorted with anguish. She took Jua into her arms. Jua could feel how thin they were. Her mom cried out again: "Jua!"

"Jelly," said the cat. The cat was sitting in front of her; she was half-awake but still looking straight into the cat's eyes. Jelly wasn't sure when the cat had come after her. Jelly's eyes found their focus. She looked around but she could no longer see the hem of her mom's dress or feel her arms holding her. All that remained was the name "Jua" and her mom's hairpin. She stuck the pin to her head. The shiny purple pin went well with the transparent pink of her body.

Jelly pressed down harder on the pin so that it wouldn't fall from her head. Then she looked at the cat, blinking her large eyes. As always, the cat was by her side. But now there was a big empty bubble inside her—one that the cat couldn't fill. The inside of the thin bubble was completely empty and cold. Jelly needed something that would fill that void. Jelly said to the cat,

"Someone told me my name is Jua."

"Jua," the cat said softly. Jelly liked the sound of the cat's familiar voice.

"Cat, I think I used to be a human. I remember so clearly how my mom hugged me and called my name. I wonder where she went," Jelly said.

The cat didn't say anything in reply. Jelly went on mumbling to herself.

"I wonder what happened. How did I turn into jelly?"

Still no reply from the cat. The yellow eyes seemed to be looking very far off into the distance. Jelly asked carefully, "I want to find my mom. Will you help me?"

<u>8</u>

The cat looked into Jelly's eyes, which were brimming with tears. She wasn't surprised by Jelly's confession. She felt as though the fish bone that had been stuck in her throat had finally gone down.

She pondered on the two names, Jelly and Jua. Jelly was Jelly—how had she suddenly turned into Jua? Couldn't she just stay as Jelly? The cat remembered the girl named Jua. The girl had cried a lot and was the one who had melted away along with her mother in the square. She had been the start of the jelly disaster in the theme park.

"You'll see, something fun is about to happen."

The cat recalled the raspy voice of the man saying those words. She didn't want to think about what had happened that day anymore. It was nothing but a nightmare. She didn't want

Jelly to find out what had happened. If the memory would only bring her pain, it was better to keep it buried. The cat looked at Jelly, who seemed to be in distress. A mix of big and little bubbles kept rising in her round body, like a carbonated drink.

"I need to find my mom. Will you help me?" Jelly asked.

In the end, there would be no one and nothing left anyway. Hiding her bitterness, the cat said with sincerity, "I just want you to be happy."

Jelly replied, saying, "I want you to be happy, too."

The cat rose to her feet and stretched. She took a deep breath, and the cold night air filled her lungs. She wanted to show Jelly right then and there the most beautiful sight she had ever seen. Something that Jelly—not Jua, but Jelly—had probably never seen before. Looking Jelly in the eyes, the cat said, "I want to show you something interesting. Come with me."

The cat led Jelly to the control booth of the carousel. Dust had settled on some of the surfaces, but it was mostly clean because it was close to the humans' boxes and had therefore been cleaned before anything else. Not only that, the carousel was the only ride in the theme park that had power—something the cat had learned while eavesdropping on the humans during the day. She jumped onto the windowsill and pointed to a red button.

"Press this," she said to Jelly.

Jelly climbed up onto the machine and stood before the button. When they had first met, Jelly hadn't even be able to climb up benches, but now she had no problem climbing up onto high places. It felt strange. Reaching out an arm toward the button, Jelly asked, "What is it?"

"Something nice will happen if you press it."

The New Seoul Park Jelly Massacre

"Something nice," Jelly said in a quiet voice as she pressed down hard on the button. Soon, the carousel began to move with a sound. The music, mixed with static noise, rang throughout the park, and the lightbulbs lit up. Jelly's eyes opened wide in wonder.

"It's so pretty …"

Jelly marveled at the sight, her eyes busy looking at the colorful lights. Sitting by her side, the cat watched the carousel going around. Something told her that she would remember this moment for a very long time to come in her long, long life.

9

Sajun made an effort to close his eyes. His mind was awfully clear. As he tossed this way and that, cheerful music penetrated his weary thoughts. It was the music of the carousel—a sound he was all too familiar with. Faint light shone in through the curtain. He pushed the curtain aside in irritation. The carousel in the square was going around and around by itself.

The music, too bright and cheerful, felt eerie somehow. But he knew he wasn't just hearing things because the other employees were beginning to wake up one by one in bewilderment. Sajun stared out the window with his sunken eyes. Some people came out running from another container and headed to the carousel in groups.

"Huh?" Sajun exclaimed, noticing something as he watched the people. He jumped to his feet and ran outside. He ran toward the bright lights as though bewitched. He felt that he was being baited but couldn't stop.

The carousel stopped on its own before the people got to it. It seemed as though it was mocking them. The people who had been moving toward it began to step back slowly and then returned to their containers. Sajun was the only one left in the square. He began walking toward the motionless carousel.

Sajun looked into the blank eyes of the horses. The chill of the early morning enveloped him; he had nothing but his pajamas on, but he didn't feel cold. He felt strangely agitated. Gasping for breath, he stared at the one who had brought him here: the cat, who was sitting in the control booth of the carousel. Clenching his teeth, he muttered, "That damn cat again ..."

It was the tuxedo cat he had run into before, the annoying little Dream Kitty. Whenever he found himself seeing things, or when things weren't going well for him, the cat would be there. She was there when he had worked as Dream Teddy too. The damn cat had sat there with a mocking look on her face as he danced in the blazing sun and suffered all sorts of hardships.

He began to approach the cat, thinking that this time he would do something about her. The cat was standing on the stairs that led up to the control booth, trying to move something with her paws. She tugged at the thing with her paws, then with her mouth, trying to pull it out. Then to Sajun's great surprise, a lump of pink jelly came into view. He could not believe his eyes.

The surface of the lump, which was about the same size as the cat, was moving up and down, as if it was breathing on its own. The edge of its base touching the ground was wriggling busily about—like a living organism. On the back of its head clung articles of various sorts. One of the articles gleamed in the darkness. It was his cell phone, for which he had searched everywhere.

"Am I seeing things?"

Frozen to the spot, he stared at the ludicrous scene. He rubbed his eyes. It was definitely jelly—one that was alive and moving. It even had blinking eyes. Sajun recalled the horrible sight he had faced upon returning from burying Yeongdu's body. That nightmare, which he had barely managed to keep buried, had now become a reality, and it began to gnaw at him. He wondered how much Yeongdu's body must have decomposed. He felt as though Yeongdu had left a curse on him.

Yeongdu's face—with his red eyes wide open even when he was being buried—became embedded in his mind. His hands trembling, Sajun grabbed his hair. He wanted to scream but nothing came out of his mouth, as if something was blocking his throat. His breathing grew faster, and his head began to spin. *This is a curse,* he mumbled in his mind. He repeated the words over and over again.

In the meantime, the cat and the lump of jelly had grown distant and had disappeared into the darkness. Looking into the blackness that surrounded him, Sajun resolved that he would not let Yeongdu ruin his life. Whatever that thing was, he would get his phone back. His bloodshot eyes glinted in the darkness.

10

The lightbulbs on the carousel flickered, changing colors: red, yellow, green. Whenever the bright colors shone into Jelly's eyes, strange images flashed through her mind. She remembered coming across the magnificent carousel before. It had been an extremely hot day. Sweating profusely, she had gone around the same area over and over again, just like the carousel, looking for her mom.

Jelly felt the cat shaking her, but she could not move. Listening to the endlessly repeating music, she wandered through her past memories, giving herself up to the flow like a leaf floating on water.

Her mom's crisp blue dress; Yuji's small, clammy hand passing her a wet tissue; the blazing sun of a hot summer day; the mushroom-shaped Lost Children Center; the employee at the center that had sounded friendly but had looked annoyed; the names announced over the speakers; the feel of her mom's damp body against hers as her mom suddenly appeared and took her into her arms; the taste of the sweet smoothie her mom had bought for her; a cat watching her from afar. What had happened after that …?

The carousel came to a stop. In the darkness that quietly settled around her, Jelly remembered the scenes that had ensued. The memories that flooded over her like a rapid torrent engulfed her—the memories were of her last moments with her mom. She vividly recalled her body growing heavier. Her mom had been touching her, but she hadn't been able to feel her hand. She had felt so sad that she had buried her face in her mom's back. And then everything had begun to crumble …

The New Seoul Park Jelly Massacre

11

The carousel, rusted and its paint peeling off, kept going around tirelessly. Jelly's eyes sparkled brightly.

A little later, lights began to go on in the boxes in which the humans lived. The humans came pouring out, looking frightened. The sound of them rushing about grew louder. The cat tapped Jelly in order to warn her. But Jelly showed no response. Her eyes were fixed on the carousel.

The sound of human footsteps grew closer. The cat hastily turned off the power and rolled Jelly, who still wasn't moving, into the control booth and hid. The carousel, going merrily around just moments before, came to a sudden stop. Again, the cat shook Jelly.

"Jelly, we need to run."

Jelly blinked her eyes slowly, as though she were submerged in water. The cat came out of the box, pushing and rolling Jelly, who still hadn't come to her senses. It was no easy task to move Jelly, as she was as big as the cat herself. It would have been much easier if she could hold Jelly in her mouth, but the soft and squashy Jelly would just droop onto the ground whenever she tried. After the cat had somehow managed to hide Jelly behind a fence near Mirrorland, she turned and watched the square, sparkling in the distance. The lights in the containers went out—it seemed the commotion had subsided.

Then came the sound of someone behind her. The cat turned around to look. The human, with a sinister look on his face, was the one she had seen inside the furry creature.

"Give me my phone, you little devil!" he screamed hysterically.

The cat looked around quickly. It was a good thing that she had hidden Jelly behind the fence. She had to get the human as far away from here as possible. She saw Mirrorland. The cat ran toward it and cried loudly on purpose. After looking around, the human fixed his gaze on the cat. He began to run, screaming savagely. The cat glanced back at Jelly behind the fence before swiftly jumping into Mirrorland.

The human came chasing after her, making strange sounds. The things he spat out sounded more like a beast's howl than human speech. Jumping over the shards of a broken mirror, the cat wondered how things had come to this. One thought led to another, then finally, she remembered Jelly's words.

"I'm not going to leave you."

That was where it had all begun. *Well, what can you do,* the cat thought. The world was full of things you had no control over, the first and foremost being your heart. Your heart wasn't completely yours once you shared it with someone. They had all left—the old woman, her daughter, and the humans who had melted away that day. In the end, she was the only one who had remained. She was always the one who was left alone with all the memories. What was the use of living for a very long time if she couldn't even keep her own heart safe?

The cat ran through the maze of countless reflections of herself. Then she came to a dead end. She saw Sajun with his bloodshot eyes in the broken mirror in front of her. He was holding a loudly roaring vacuum cleaner. Its long tube that reached up to the human's waist and its wide-open mouth looking threatening.

The cat turned around and glared at Sajun. Jelly's voice

hovered in her ears. As soon as those words had touched her ears, she had somehow known that this moment would come. She could finally accept that fact. The human approached her slowly, raising the vacuum cleaner high. The curse-like words that spilled out of his mouth echoed throughout Mirrorland.

12

Someone was screaming. Jelly wasn't sure if it was herself, her mom, or someone else. Feeling drowsy, she curled up into a ball. At that moment, a clear voice penetrated through her memories. Her eyes lit up and her drifting mind settled back into place. She came to and looked around. The cat wasn't there.

"Cat! Cat!" she called out.

She remembered watching the carousel go around with the cat by her side, but for some reason she was now behind a fence on the path to Mirrorland. Jelly went outside and called out to the cat. But what she heard back was a fierce shriek. The sound came from inside Mirrorland. Jelly moved as quickly as she could, dragging her heavy body. As she entered Mirrorland, she heard a familiar whirring sound and the sound of a human speaking.

"You little devil! You think you'll get your way? Where's my phone?" the human screamed.

Jelly slid through the maze of mirrors and saw the back of the human's head just ahead of her. Clinging to a wall, she poked her head out and tried to get a grasp of the situation. The three walls were covered with mirrors. In the middle of the room, the human was pointing the mouth of the vacuum monster at the cat.

Jelly fought back a scream. The cat glared at the human, baring her teeth, her fur bristling.

Jelly stared at the vacuum monster's mouth. The darkness inside the gaping hole seemed unfathomable. Countless jellies had been sucked up into that hole. She, too, would probably get eaten by the monster. She hid behind the mirror trembling, and again, the cat yowled. This time, though, it sounded different. Jelly's eyes met the cat's yellow eyes in the mirror. With her eyes pointing to the entrance, the cat was signaling to Jelly that she should run.

Wiping away her tears, Jelly came out from behind the wall of mirror. She couldn't run away by herself and leave the cat here. She climbed up the highest circular mirror. Seeing her, the human opened his eyes wide and shouted, "M-my cell phone!"

Jelly shut her eyes tight and flung herself down. It was the biggest leap she had ever taken. Having landed safely on the human's face, she spread herself out and wrapped her body around his head. The human shook the monster's long mouth in the air. Bracing herself, Jelly cried out, "Stop harassing the cat!"

The vacuum cleaner fell from the human's hands. He dug forcefully into Jelly's body with both hands. Jelly held out, her eyes closed. Her body stretched out like dough but would not break. The human's hook-like hand, scratching violently at her, snatched at the phone that was stuck to her side.

The human struggled like a fish snatched out of the sea. His arms, wildly flapping around, made the hairpin fall to the ground. Looking at the pin bouncing off the floor, Jelly barely managed to stifle her tears. Time passed. The human gradually stopped moving. His body, drained of energy, fell back helplessly. His head fell on a shard of glass with a thud. Jelly opened her eyes at last. Her back was ragged from the human's scratching and pulling. Red liquid came leaking out of the human's head. Jelly dragged her stretched-out body down to the floor. The cat came up to her and asked, "Are you all right?"

The cat's yellow eyes calmed her trembling heart. Slowly, Jelly nodded her head. The human remained still, his eyes wide open. His pale hands were gripping the phone. Jelly gave up trying to pry the phone out of his hand and started moving away. Jelly and the cat walked in silence. When they came out of Mirrorland together, the sun was rising over the mountain.

_13_

Jelly and the cat returned to the café and laid down deep in a drawer. They were overcome with exhaustion but couldn't sleep. The cat saw what a mess Jelly had become—she had always been as round as a drop of water, but now she was like a lump of kneaded dough. *You should've run when I told you to,* the cat thought, licking Jelly's uneven surface. She tasted bittersweet. Jelly twisted and turned, her eyes closed. The cat recalled the look on Jelly's face when she had been watching the carousel go around. The cat blinked slowly. She wished that Jelly would stop chasing her memories.

A loud siren tore the cat out of her shallow sleep. She poked her head out of the drawer and saw several cars outside the window. Red lights were flashing on top of the cars. The same red light had shone when the old woman had died. So the death of the old woman was the same thing as the death of this human.

Two different people had died, but there was the same sound ringing and the same light shining. The cat recalled the old woman's body, which was carried off somewhere, and the brick house that had become empty—the house without anyone inside, the house without a sound.

It suddenly occurred to her that she could end up alone again. The cat looked at Jelly lying next to her. In just a few hours, Jelly's body had returned to normal, and it now looked like a drop of water with a smooth surface again. Jelly was fast asleep, as if to say that she didn't care about the sirens or the human commotion. Lying by her side, the cat, too, gently closed her eyes.

14

Jelly had a long, long dream. Her memories had come to her a piece at a time like a puzzle and now unfolded in their proper order. At last, Jelly could fully accept the fact that Jua's memories were her own—even the memory of her mom screaming in that final moment.

Jelly turned over. Warm sunlight poured in through the window all the way into the drawer. Jelly examined her body, which was no longer human. Was she still Jua when she had changed so much? Could she still be Jua? Amid the confusion brought on by her changed body and newly recalled memories, she was sure of one thing. She wanted to see her mom.

The cat was sleeping late, which wasn't like her. Jelly slid carefully out of the drawer, trying not to wake her. She made her way cautiously out of the café and moved through the flowerbed so that the humans wouldn't see her.

She saw Mirrorland in the distance. Unusually, there was yellow tape around it and quite a lot of people. She felt uneasy, remembering what had happened the day before. She shook her head as if to shake off the memory. Across from her, there were humans with vacuum cleaners as usual. Staying away from Mirrorland, she chased after the busily moving humans. She intended to keep an eye on them all day to find out what happened to all the jellies that disappeared.

When the appointed hour came, the humans headed somewhere carrying their vacuum cleaners and trash bins. The answer probably lay where they went. Following them with her eyes, Jelly furtively attached herself to the bottom of the trash bin that was carried by the man last in line. She could hear the humans talking nearby.

"Have you heard the rumor that the jellies here come alive and move around at night like zombies?

"What? How can jellies move around? It's not like they're game characters or something."

"And there was something weird about the guy who died yesterday—the contract worker."

"What creeps me out the most is that this place is opening up again."

Jelly could hear the sound of dozens of wheels rolling on the ground. She clung to the bottom of the bin, not wanting to fall. The bin soon came to a stop. As the human played on his phone, looking bored, Jelly quickly hid herself in a nearby pile of trash.

The humans lined up in front of a huge garbage truck. The truck was even taller than the humans and had a long ladder fixed to the side. The humans took turns climbing up the ladder and dumping out everything in their bins. All kinds of things—not just jelly, but bags, watches, shoes, and T-shirts—fell out at once.

When the humans had all left and the sun was beginning to set, Jelly crawled out of the pile of trash. She stood in the middle of the road, staring up at the huge truck. So this was where all the jellies that had been sucked up by the vacuum cleaners had ended up. Her mom was sure to be at the place where the truck was headed. Slowly, Jelly started making her way toward the truck.

"Don't go," the cat said from behind her.

15

The cat stared at the round body of Jelly, who seemed so distant. Since when had she started going around alone? In the beginning, Jelly had clung to her so much that it had annoyed her. The cat wished that things could go back to the way they once were. But she knew, of course, that it was impossible.

"I'm not going to leave you."

It might have been those words, in the end, that led to this moment. She should not have trusted someone who had once been human. They always came and left so easily. All she could do was accept things as they were. But this time, at least, she could raise her voice and say something. She approached Jelly, who was staring up at the dump truck.

"Don't go," she said.

Jelly turned around. That round body and those round eyes. She was the same as she had been when they first met.

The cat went on to say, "I want you to be happy—here with me, for a long time. It's even scarier out there. It's full of things more terrifying than vacuum cleaners."

She didn't want to let Jelly go. She didn't think she could stand being alone again, or live any longer in the chill of the old brick house. Sadness, a feeling which she had forgotten for a long time, reared its head. The cat looked Jelly in the face. Jelly's pink form looked orange in the sunset. She looked much stronger than when she was pink. Jelly opened her mouth slowly and said, "I'm sorry, Cat, that I can't keep my promise about not leaving you."

The cat had known this was coming, but she couldn't keep her heart from sinking.

"I have to go. I have to find my mom, like she found me," Jelly said and came slowly up to her. The cat looked calmly at Jelly. Jelly took the hairpin from her head. She reached out her little arm and scooped up a part of herself, placed the bit of jelly on the cat's neck, and put the pin there. The hairpin clung to the cat, as though it had been glued on.

"Thank you for everything, Cat," Jelly said.

The cat raised a paw in reply. She barely managed to hold back her tears. Then she pressed down on Jelly's head with her paw and left a pawprint, just like the first time they had met. The pawprint would fade away with time, but she hoped that the memory, at least, wouldn't fade away so easily.

Jelly turned around and headed to the dump truck. She began to climb up the ladder. The hairpin on the cat's fur swayed this way and that in the chilly night breeze. The cat sat with her paws together, watching Jelly as she climbed up the ladder.

Though Jelly slipped and missed her footing now and then, she eventually managed to get to the top of the dump truck. After standing there for a long time, Jelly turned her head and looked the cat in the eyes. She seemed to be saying goodbye.

16

Holding onto the rail of the ladder, Jelly stared at the deep inside of the truck. It was full of pink jelly like her. She turned her head for the last time and locked eyes with the cat. The cat's shiny yellow eyes sparkled. Jelly opened her mouth slightly and said in a very faint voice, "Goodbye."

Jelly was sure that the cat had heard. She threw herself into the truck. A deep darkness engulfed her, and something that felt similar to her own body warmly embraced her. It felt so snug. Jelly closed her eyes.

New Seoul Park

*

A tense atmosphere pervaded the Seoul Public Officials Training Center. People were talking in groups of twos and threes, excited and nervous at the same time. A woman spoke up, saying, "Aren't there a lot more additional people from the waiting list than usual? I heard that normally no more than ten people give up their place, but this year ... I don't even know how many did."

All eyes turned to the woman who had casually brought up this taboo subject. The woman smiled. She had brought it up precisely for that reason—she enjoyed the attention.

"Yeah, I heard that there's even someone who disappeared, you know, in that incident."

Despite the caution in his voice, the tone of the conversation was as light as a feather. One of the men who had been listening said, scratching his head, "I got in from the waiting list because of that. I barely passed—otherwise I would've had to prepare for another year."

"Oh, yeah? Me too, actually."

"Oh, really?"

The mood brightened instantly. The people, there to be rewarded after long periods of hard work, smiled as they pictured a secure future unfolding before them. They didn't have any extra energy left to really think about those who hadn't been able to come to take their place for some unavoidable reason, even though they had passed. On the wall in front of them hung a large banner that read: "Congratulations, Seoul City Officials!"

Everyone took a picture together with big smiles on their faces.

*

Hi everyone, it's me, Haru. Our topic today has propelled this channel to the top trending list. You know what the topic is, right? "The true identity of Yu Hyeongyeong, the head of Gwangnan Cleaning!"

Yu disappeared all of a sudden about two months ago. Some speculate that she was involved in "the incident." As for me, I'm one hundred percent sure that she was. Which raises the question: Why did Yu go to the theme park that day? And all by herself, too. What, to enjoy the rides? An incredibly busy CEO visits a theme park on the weekend, just because she wants to have some fun alone?

I came across some incredible information a while ago. Remember my raid on a religious cult a while back? Well, someone there told me about this site. I got curious so I checked it out. You know how crazy I am about mysteries. The registration process was extremely complicated. And guess what—it turned out to be a devil worship site. It was weird. And creepy. It was this site right here. You can see it on the screen, right?

Now, look at this post here. You can see that there are two members that are revered by the others and are most famous on the site: Sodok and Jelly Bean. Cute nicknames, huh? Well, these two seem to have always fought like cats and dogs. But after the incident, they both stopped posting. Which got me curious again. So I stayed up all night going through their previous posts.

And if you look at the posts by Sodok ... Okay, this one right here. Do you see this photo? It's a photo of a hotel room. You see that bit of the TV screen in the corner? Take a good look, and you'll see a reflection of someone there. If you zoom in like this ... Here, doesn't that look like Yu Hyeongyeong?

*

The girl was feeling great after the get-together with her former classmates from the education institute that she hadn't seen in a while. She opened the door, slurring her words as she spoke, and her roommate welcomed her in. Her roommate was a teacher at a nearby middle school; the two had met in Noryangjin. People usually lost touch after their exams without even saying goodbye, but she and her roommate had kept up their friendship.

In Noryangjin, passing an exam meant goodbye. So everyone there wanted to be able to say goodbye. She remembered that one guy from her class had a girlfriend preparing for a teacher certification exam and had cheated on her after he passed his primary examination. Jaeyun, was it? He hadn't shown up at the get-together. Had he failed the interview? Or perhaps he had passed and gotten a post outside of Seoul.

Well, in any case, there was no need to dwell on Noryangjin

anymore since she had passed her exam. Her roommate was under a lot of stress lately and often drank beer at home—she wasn't a big drinker so one can of beer was enough to get her drunk. Her roommate, shaking the can of beer in her hand and with her face somewhat flushed, asked, "You want one?"

"Sure," the girl replied, thinking one more can wouldn't do her any harm. She took out a beer from the fridge. The can opened with a refreshing pop. It reminded her of the sound of waves. The two clinked their cans together in a toast like always. Then they chatted about the get-together and what happened at school that day.

Her roommate, who finished her beer first, said in an annoyed voice, "Something ridiculous happened today. One of the kids in my class wouldn't hand over his phone. You know how I've been put in charge of this class as a homeroom teacher, which is totally unexpected and ridiculous because specialist teachers aren't usually assigned a homeroom. One of the English teachers in our school went missing, so I've been temporarily assigned. It's so annoying. I hate kids. But I mean, I still have to work, so I took his phone away for a little while because he kept staring at it and chuckling during class. I wondered what he was looking at so I checked his phone, and the screen showed some weird site with eerie drawings. And all the popular posts at the top had strange titles—you know, about devil worship and stuff like that. The kind of stuff that's been on TV a few times lately. Devil worship? In this country? Yeah, right. How likely is that? But then I saw the kid glaring at me, the whites of his eyes showing … It gave me the creeps! So I just gave the phone back to him. Kids today are so scary. You never know what they might do."

"How long are you in charge of them?"

"Oh, just till the end of this week. They've hired a new temp."

Her roommate tipped the remaining beer into her mouth. Then the beer was gone. The girl glanced at the blaring television in the living room. A current affairs program that was playing at the barbecue restaurant she had been at earlier today was playing again.

"That's odd," she said.

"What is?" her roommate asked.

"I saw that earlier at the restaurant today. Do they usually air the same show over and over again like this on the same day?"

"Well, maybe, since it's cable TV," her roommate said.

The girl nodded. The producer of the program was headed to New Seoul Park. The theme park, which was situated deep in some mountains, looked dismal. There was a sign hanging on the entrance saying, TO BE REOPENED SOON. Her roommate turned off the television with the remote.

The two went into their separate rooms. In the darkness of her room, the girl turned on her laptop. The black website that had featured on the current affairs program was flickering on her screen. The log-in window popped up over the spinning black cauldron. She entered her ID and password and scrolled through the popular posts with a bored look on her face. The more recent posts flashed on the screen.

"Is it true that Sodok is the head of Gwangnan Cleaning? That's crazy!"

"Her ID makes perfect sense now."

"The newbies have turned this site into a mess. And there aren't that many posts anymore."

"I almost got my phone confiscated for reading posts today. I was so pissed off."

"So that's what happened with her. What about Jelly Bean? Why doesn't he post anymore?"

The last post was getting real-time comments on it.

"So Jelly Bean was right after all."

"Please come back, Jelly Bean."

"When will the next Sabbath be?"

The girl kept the site open and opened a new browser window over it. Then she did some online searching. She then returned to the site and pressed the "Write" button. She kept on writing and deleting her words. Soon, a new post was made. On her little desk was a packet of jelly and grains of sugar.

"I saw something weird today, in a sewer around a subway station. It looked like jelly but it was moving. It was nasty, so I ran."

She had never seen such a thing. Moving jelly? What rubbish. But her post got some comments, a lot of them actually, which hadn't happened in a while. Even the comments telling her not to lie made her happy. She smiled.

*

A strange rumor began to spread through the city like a fad. It was a virus—it sneaked up on people, spreading further and further. Everyone heard different stories and pictured different figures and different outcomes. But in the end, they were all forgotten, just like a common cold virus.

All the stories were vague, but one of them had some substance and clarity to it: it was a video uploaded on a streaming site. The low-resolution video showed a mysterious lump wriggling around in a corner. The lump slowly crawled up the ladder of a dump truck like a worm and plunged into the back of the truck.

The video closely zoomed in on the mysterious lump of jelly before ending. Then an interview came on with tacky captions. A man, whose face was blurred and also covered with a cute emoticon, was speaking in a poorly disguised voice. He identified himself as a former cleaner working for a subcontractor of New Seoul Park.

"The rides would start moving all of a sudden in the middle of the night, but then they would stop immediately if we went up to them. It was spooky. There was also a kid who died while working ... Oh, wait, I shouldn't have said that. You can edit that, right?"

The number of views had skyrocketed. People from different areas cropped up, saying that they had seen lumps of moving jelly. A visit to New Seoul Park—a sort of test of courage—was considered a must for online broadcasters. The question of who could make the scariest and yet most enjoyable video from generally similar material became the determining factor for the number of views.

One of the broadcasters got lost in the mountain surrounding the park while chasing Dream Kitty after he had found her near the Hamster Wheel. Later on, a post was uploaded saying that he saw the ghost of a very thin man, but no one took him seriously, which of course was usually the case with ghost stories.

The fad died down as quickly as it had spread. A decisive moment was when a meddlesome television program called in an expert who proved that the video was a hoax. The person who had first started circulating the video adamantly denied it but said nothing more when an article came out saying that the interviewee—the former cleaner—had been sued by Gwangnan Cleaning and New Seoul Park for libel and breach of contract. Disappointed, people turned their attention elsewhere. Something new and sensational happened every day. The story was soon forgotten.

*

Six months passed. A sea of people came gathering at the entrance of New Seoul Park, which was now reopening. They were loud and full of energy, as if to say that nothing awful had ever happened in the first place or that something so depressing and absurd shouldn't have ever happened.

The new part-timers in their mascot costumes were dancing vivaciously near the line of waiting people. The big screen in the parking lot was streaming an endless array of flashy commercials celebrating the reopening of New Seoul Park. And Dream Teddy, of course, was dancing with his friends in front of the screen, sending balloons up into the air.

"Free tickets to celebrate the park's reopening!" they shouted.

Firecrackers went off. Children laughed and several employees, looking tense with their ears plugged, went on with the preparations for the opening. Loud music pumped out from the large speakers at both sides of the small stage. The surface of the ground around it seemed to be shaking. A ribbon-cutting ceremony was held, with smoke from the front of the stage and tiny pieces of colored paper floating around in the air. Dream Teddy and his friends cut the red ribbon tied across the entrance with great enthusiasm.

The crowd cheered. Their cries echoed for a long time through the mountain behind the theme park.

"The park is now open!"

With these words, people flocked to the entrance like a swarm of bees. But then the energy and excitement from before took a different turn. People could be heard swearing and shouting at one another to not push and shove. They kept rushing forward as though zombies were chasing after them. Cries were muffled by the commotion. It seemed that someone had fallen and was injured, but they had disappeared beneath the feet of the crowd. An increasing number of children were crying as they got shoved and stepped on. It was impossible to tell exactly where the line had become disorderly. The music coming from the big screen and the speakers was still as cheerful as ever.

A pair of eyes watched the scene in silence. There was a figure standing still in a corner of the parking lot, wearing only the head of a mascot costume. A little boy standing at a distance from the crowd, too scared to squeeze his way in, tugged at his mother's sleeve. The mother, having watched the throng of people with an anxious look on her face, sighed and turned her head to look at the boy. The boy pointed somewhere with his finger.

"Mom, why isn't that Dream Teddy dancing? Why is he standing still?"

The mother turned around to see, but there was no one there.

"You must be seeing things. Hold my hand tight—you don't want to get lost," she said.

The little boy turned around to look once again, reluctant to leave. Dream Teddy was there again. The boy blinked his round eyes. Dream Teddy waved his hands cheerfully toward the boy, who smiled brightly and waved back. There was nothing beyond the gaping holes of Dream Teddy's eyes.

The Missing Child

Yuji opened her eyes with a scream. A bright and cold light pierced her eyes. Someone handed her a cup of juice as she sat there in a cold sweat.

"Someone reported you—you were asleep outside in front of the police station. Did you run away from home?" asked a man.

The man was in a police uniform. Yuji took a quick look around. She couldn't see anyone melting or hear anyone screaming. She was at a perfectly ordinary police station. She blinked her eyes slowly, and the scenes she had witnessed at the theme park seemed to fade far away into the distance. Maybe it had all been a dream. Maybe she had just had a very long, terrible nightmare. She felt sluggish, as though her senses hadn't fully returned. She touched her skin with her trembling hands. It was cold from long exposure to the air conditioner, but it wasn't squishy or sticky. She heaved a sigh of relief.

It was ridiculous, when she thought about it. People melting because they ate some strange jelly? And most of all, there was no way that her mom and dad would have left her at the theme park, no matter how bad things were between them. Yuji drank the juice the policeman had given her in one gulp. The nice, cold drink slid down her throat. After she finished her juice down to the last drop, she noticed something; her ankle, sticking out from under a blanket, was covered in pink spots. She ran her fingers over her ankle and found that they were sticky.

The police officers had been watching the television in the corner but suddenly started talking in loud whispers. Yuji fixed her eyes on the television showing the news. The news anchor was delivering some breaking news in an agitated tone.

"The pink liquid has been identified as fruit-flavored jelly. All electronic equipment in the area was out of operation at the estimated time of the incident. Further investigation is necessary to pinpoint the connection between the jelly explosion at the theme park and the large-scale disappearance ..."

The screen showed a panorama of the theme park covered in pink jelly. Looking dazed, Yuji pinched herself. It hurt, so it wasn't a dream. If everything she had been through had actually happened, she had a question—a question that had tormented her until the very last moment before she had passed out. Where were her mom and dad?

"Your parents are home," said a voice in her ear.

Yuji looked around. The police officer had gone off with the empty cup. But she was sure that someone had whispered in her ear. Yuji recalled the man she had seen at the theme park in that final moment. His strange, raspy voice hovered in her mind like a never-ending song. He alone had been fine while everyone else had melted away. She had seen him face to face, but for some reason she couldn't remember what he looked like at all.

The New Seoul Park Jelly Massacre

Her head began to throb. The only thing she remembered clearly from that day ... were the whites of Jua's eyes.

"Yuji, my mom and I are one now."

Now that she had remembered, the eyes wouldn't leave her mind. Yuji shook her head vigorously. Some of the officers came up to her and asked if she was all right, but she shrugged them away and ran out of the police station. She had come out of the theme park, but she was still in a nightmare.

Yuji input the passcode for the door and went inside. A chilling silence greeted her. The door to the study opened and a black shadow came walking out. It was her dad. Frowning, he came toward her.

"Where have you been?" he asked.

Where have you been? She was the one who wanted to ask that. Confused, Yuji stared at him. She wondered for a moment if it had all been a dream after all, but the news she had seen at the police station had been real. Her dad looked a little tired but no different from usual. But something was off. No, everything was off. Her dad didn't look at all like someone fretting over a missing daughter. Yuji didn't know what to say. Soon, her mom came running out of the master bedroom.

"Yuji, is that you? Where have you been? You should've told us where you were going!"

Yuji opened her mouth with difficulty.

"I was at the theme park ..." She began.

Immediately, the faces of her parents crumpled, as though they had seen something awful. Her mom grabbed Yuji by the shoulders and demanded, "Didn't you come home with your dad in the car? Don't lie to me now!"

Yuji timidly shook her head no. Her mom leapt to her feet and glared at Yuji's dad. Then her familiar, screechy voice filled the air.

"What is she saying? Has she really been at the theme park all this time? You told me that she came in the car with you. You told me she came home, then went out to play!"

"She did come with me. I even found the packet of jelly she was playing with in the car. I kept getting distracted by the rustling sound and ended up getting lost around the same road over and over again!"

"But what is she saying then? Are you saying that she's lying?"

"Like I said, I thought she went out to play straight after coming home. And what gives you the right to blame me? Let's be honest here, you're the one who got mad and stalked off alone! Yuji, how did you get home? And don't lie to us!"

"Don't yell at her. Yuji, tell us what happened. You shouldn't shock grown-ups like this."

Silence fell. Their fierce gazes seemed to bore into Yuji. She backed away, looking from one pair of bloodshot eyes to the other. Her parents resumed shouting and bombarding her with questions. This wasn't what she had wanted to hear. She curled up in a corner and covered her ears.

Her parents stopped fighting only after several calls of complaint came in from the neighbors, and they went into their room. Yuji sat all alone in the dark living room. She noticed a packet of jelly on the table in front of the sofa. There was a yellow envelope placed neatly next to the packet of jelly. Sheets of white paper were sticking out of it, calling for attention.

Slowly, Yuji pulled out the sheets of paper. A blood-red seal was stamped in a corner. It was their divorce papers. Yuji realized at last that her parents were so thoroughly torn apart that they could no longer be put back together with something so flimsy as tape. Yuji—who had once served as the tape—was, in truth, nothing but one of the reasons why they had become torn apart.

She reached for the jelly. The packet was already torn open, so she didn't need to fumble with it noisily. She grabbed a handful of the sticky lumps and put them in her mouth. She sucked on them for a while, then chewed down on them. Melted jelly stuck between her teeth. She could clearly hear the sound of her jaw creaking as she chewed and the sound of the jelly being crushed by her teeth. The apartment was unbearably quiet without her parents fighting.

With the packet of jelly in her hand, Yuji slowly walked over to her parents' room. She turned the knob and pushed the door open, and saw her mom and dad lying with their backs to each other. They seemed to be pushing each other away, like the same pole magnets she had seen in a textbook at school. The scene of Jua and her mom hugging each other kept replaying in her mind. She was tormented by the image of the two. They who looked so much alike that it was almost scary, they who hugged each other so closely that there was no space for another. Yuji bit her lip fiercely. The taste of blood mixed with the sweetness of the jelly.

Looking at her cold-hearted parents with their backs to each other, Yuji wished that they would cling to each other like Jua and her mom. She put all the jelly in her hand into her mouth. Grains of sugar fell to the floor, and a sweet smell assailed her nose. Her mouth full of jelly, Yuji squeezed in between her parents.

Lying between the two of them, Yuji stared up at the ceiling. The pattern on the ceiling of the old apartment became strangely contorted. Before she knew it, the pattern had turned into the jelly vendor's face, melting as it looked down at her. His mouth, a black hole, tore open, and his raspy voice pervaded the room. Yuji chewed the jelly in her mouth as hard as she could. The sweetness spread from her tongue throughout her body. When all the jelly in her mouth had lost its shape, Yuji closed her eyes, feeling her melted fingernails trickling down her fingers.

The New Seoul Park Jelly Massacre

honfordstar.com